by
CAT BAUER

HARLEY'S NINTH

Alfred A. Knopf new york

THIS IS A BORZOI BOOK PUBLISHED BY ALFRED A. KNOPF

Published in the United States by Alfred A. Knopf, an imprint of Random House Children's Books, a division of Random House, Inc., New York.

KNOPF, BORZOI BOOKS, and the colophon are registered trademarks of Random House, Inc.

www.randomhouse.com/teens

Educators and librarians, for a variety of teaching tools, visit us at www.randomhouse.com/teachers

Library of Congress Cataloging-in-Publication Data
Bauer, Cat.
Harley's ninth / by Cat Bauer. — 1st ed.
    p.   cm.
SUMMARY: Now sixteen and living with her biological father in New York City, Harley Columba prepares for the first exhibition of her paintings under a cloud of worry that she is pregnant, while a trip to her hometown brings major surprises, both good and bad.
ISBN 978-0-375-83736-4 (trade)
ISBN 978-0-375-93736-1 (lib. bdg.)
[1. Artists—Fiction.   2. Fathers and daughters—Fiction.
3. Pregnancy—Fiction.   4. New York (N.Y.)—Fiction.]   I. Title.
PZ7.B32585Has 2007
[Fic]—dc22
2006003485

Printed in the United States of America

February 2007

10 9 8 7 6 5 4 3 2 1

First Edition

Per Paolo,
il mio equilibrio

. . . That ye, being rooted and grounded in love, may be able to comprehend with all saints what is the breadth and length and depth and height.

—Paul the Apostle

Creative writing
Mr. Alberti
Room 225
Autobiographical incident

LOVE WITH A BACH TEAR
by Harley Columba

We are on top of the bed. My father is not home. It is hard
to find a place to honor your love when you are sixteen
and there is a Nordic god right next to you. A home
without a grown-up is a moment to be stolen. This is why
we are on top of the bed.

Evan is irresistible, with arms as hard as Odin himself,
strong biceps that encompass me with shelter. He kisses
me the way he does, blond hair tumbling across my face,
gray eyes touching my insides. "I love you too much," he
says.

"I love *you* too much," I say. We laugh and he kisses
my nose. He brushes the hair off my face and kisses my
lips. The September sun crowns the back of his head with
a halo the color of bullion. Outside the window, the
sparrows on the bird feeder chirp their approval. "We have
an audience," I say.

Evan unbuttons the first tiny button on my white
summer sweater. "Let them watch."

My room is off the kitchen, more like a closet than a
bedroom, with only a futon sofa to sleep on and a skinny
dresser for my clothes; a nightstand and lamp are next to
the bed. It had been the workroom of my father, Sean

Shanahan, until I moved in with him last month, the place where he sketched his drafts—he is designing the Broadway set for *Answers*, that Nicholas Raftner play. "The man is an alchemist," Sean said. "His words turn my wood into gold." Now Sean's draft table is in his studio at the other end of the apartment, along with his scale models and the Tony Award he won for his last play. My easel is crammed into his corner; if it bothers him, he hasn't said.

On top of the dresser is my portable, playing Bach, magic music. Outside, the sparrows chirp as if they know the tune.

Evan unbuttons the second button, and then the third. I close my eyes. He moves his tongue inside my mouth, very lightly, very sweetly; it is so familiar, like going home. His hand slides under my sweater and inside my bra. His lips brush against my neck, pause, then move down, and down again. I slide my fingers like a comb through his hair and press his head against me. Sometimes he seems like a little boy when I hold him like this.

He sits up and takes off his shirt. I shrug the straps of my bra off my shoulders, spin it around, and unhook it. I put on a show. I toss my head like a fashion model, pouty lips, lion eyes. My mahogany hair spills across my shoulder; the sun hits my highlights and turns my brown curls to red. Evan laughs. He slides his hands over my breasts and holds my waist. "We need a photo."

I giggle. "Of both of us. We are too beautiful. We must preserve the memory for when we are old and fat."

"We will never be old and fat. Old, maybe, but not fat." Evan eases me onto the pillow. He kisses me again. "Oh."

This time the kisses start sweetly but transform into something other, kisses that reach past my mouth and into my depths. Our breath is quicker than time; it is another rhythm from a different heaven. Evan yanks at my belt and unfastens the buckle. He pulls down my jeans; I kick them off. He takes off his jeans, and I see he is wearing the black briefs I bought him. I am wearing the white lacy thong he bought me. He touches me. I am a river. I touch him. He is a stone.

"Do you have a rubber?"

"I'll pull out."

I hesitate. "Are you sure?"

His eyes are deep and gray. "Sure."

Danger. Danger. I should resist, but we are on top of the bed, an honorable venue, and he is like chocolate. He melts into me. The music changes. An oboe and a violin begin a duet with notes so pure, octaves direct from the sun to the moon.

I am the oboe. Evan is the violin. The violin speaks. The oboe answers. The musical instruments fill the intervals with each other's tones; the tones have matching colors. Red. Gold. Silver. Evan's body is somewhere above me; it has turned to ether; I can only smell him. . . . A light appears like a beacon, a white light tinged with violet. It is only Evan's eyes I see, and the light. His eyes connect to mine, gray to blue, and I am gone, up to the cracks between the stars.

"Harley? Harley, are you home?" Sean's voice is outside the door and I tumble back to earth.

"Damn!" Evan pulls away and leaves a puddle of consequences on my pelvis.

I grab a tissue out of the box on the nightstand and

clean myself off. I tug on my jeans and yank my sweater over my head without the bra. When my head pops out, Evan is already dressed.

"Yeah! In here!" I grab my sketch pad off the top of the dresser and flip it open.

There is a knock at the door and Sean sticks his head in. His mahogany hair is as thick as mine; his blue eyes echo my own. He sizes up the situation: Evan and I sit next to each other as if we have been there for hours. We zone in on my drawing of a wild rose like it is better than van Gogh.

"Hey, Sean." Evan looks up and tries to be casual.

"Hey, Evan." Sean grins. He has a raspy voice that sounds like the wilderness. "Am I interrupting anything?"

I hope my hair is not a shambles. "I'm just showing Evan my new sketches."

"Yeah. Right. I've used that line, too." Sean winks. I watch the thoughts reel across his face. A teenager in the house is foreign to him, and he is rusty in the discipline department. He decides on leniency. "I'll be in my studio." He slowly closes the door until it makes a soft click.

We listen to the floorboards squeak beneath Sean's footsteps as he passes through the kitchen and down the hall, and then we collapse into a huddle of silent laughter.

Today, OCTOBER 9TH

8:00 A.M.

It is the ninth and I am five days late: that is all I can think as I jog down to the Hudson River. Five days late. Five days feels like forever when you're female and linked to the whimsies of the moon.

Today happens to be John Lennon's birthday, October 9th. Sean said he would take me to an exhibit of John Lennon's artwork down in Soho that Yoko has arranged to celebrate the day. It also happens to be Saturday, which is a good thing because tomorrow is Sunday and I have another day before I have to go to my creative-writing class. I want to rewrite my paper. Now that I am five days late, a romantic interlude starring Evan seems somehow inappropriate.

I wrote my essay, "Love with a Bach Tear," when it was assigned, two weeks ago. Mr. Alberti had issued a challenge and said: "Autobiographical incident. Anything goes." My fellow seniors at my chic Manhattan school grouped together and decided we would be bold. Natasha Silver, who loves to shock, proclaimed she was going to write her own "private moment" disguised as a Georgia O'Keeffe iris. Livingston Smith said he would counter with a sonnet, "Ode to Little Livingston"—you can only imagine. They have already read theirs out loud, and both were hilarious. My new school is up front and in your face; you would be branded forever in Lenape

Lakes, New Jersey, for writing scenes like that. I was worried I wouldn't fit in with all these urbanites, but it suits me better than Lenape ever did. Everybody is weird, not just me, and at least they have a sense of humor. I wrote the part about Sean's Tony Award because Bitsy Cooley, this totally obnoxious cretin, is always going on and on about her mother's Daytime Emmy. I mean, really. Everybody has a parent in The Arts.

"Love with a Bach Tear." Using music as a metaphor might sound a little flowery, but Penelope Powell's "An Arrow Through My Heart" was mushier than mine; she is in love with a sculptor. Thank God we ran out of time on Friday; I am up first on Monday. But now, what once seemed poetic now seems prophetic, and there is no way I can read mine out loud.

The air is warm and bright, cut with a dash of autumn. I jog down West Eleventh Street past exotic nannies, already up and out, strolling rosy-cheeked babies, most of them twins. There is a plethora of twins on West Eleventh Street, as if all the women in the neighborhood gossiped over coffee at Brew Bar and decided to go to the same fertility specialist en masse. And then there is me, so fertile that I have managed to conceive outside the womb, a Harley Columba Immaculate Conception.

I push the button to cross West Street and feel the mechanical energy of the cars and trucks whizzing past me, speeding, zooming, just flooring it up to the Lincoln Tunnel and beyond. I feel powerful when the light turns yellow, then red, and forces the entire speedway to stop, a simple miracle that holds back the flood of motorized tension like Moses parting the Red Sea.

I jog across West and over the bicycle path, down to

the edge of the river. I flip one leg, then the other, over the rail directly across from the old Erie-Lackawanna Railroad trestle on the Jersey side, and stretch. Then I jog out toward the pier, keeping the Statue of Liberty, which is far, far in the distance, in my sight.

I want to achieve liberty. I want to achieve peace of mind. I want to imagine all the people living life in peace. But it is difficult to rein in your brain when you are five days late and, in addition, have your *first art exhibition in a major New York gallery tonight*, and, honestly, I am slightly hysterical.

I turn right onto the pier and jog past the freshly mowed, industrial-strength, genetically altered grass, so green and lush it seems artificial. There are white-purple clouds in the sky, ponderous and fluffy, set against a clear aqua blue backdrop; that, too, seems computer generated.

I get to the end of the pier and stop. There is a cute black guy on a walkie-talkie standing in my corner, chatting with his friend, whose name seems to be Adonis. I listen. The static is loud and Adonis is asking ridiculous questions like: "It's sunny here. Yo, Nigel. Is it sunny there?" It is not much of a conversation, and Nigel is in my sacred spot, unknowingly aligned with the torch of the Statue of Liberty beaming between the sun and moon. He is loud, he is happening; the benefits of the position don't seem to be affecting him in the least.

The irritation bubbles inside me like little goose bumps on the wrong side of my skin. I stop about five feet to the left of Nigel and hold on to the rail, but, of course, now the configuration is off; I am not in direct alignment with the torch of the Statue of Liberty and I am five days late. Then I recognize that my interior goose bumps are not goose bumps at all but strange hormones bouncing inside my body, and I am positive I am pregnant.

"Is that Staten Island? Is that Staten Island over there?" I realize that Nigel is talking to me. He is pointing to New Jersey.

"No. That's New Jersey. Staten Island is over there, past the Statue of Liberty." Apparently, Nigel is not from these parts. Apparently, he is unfamiliar with the Code of Behavior at the end of the pier, where one goes for quiet contemplation in quest of liberty and justice for all. And why has he got a walkie-talkie instead of a cell phone? The rest of the world should not have to suffer because he won't pay for a line.

"That's the Statue of Liberty? I didn't even see it! Cool." He presses a button on the walkie-talkie. "Yo, Adonis, guess what? I can see the Statue of Liberty. You gotta come out here, man. You gotta see this thing."

I take a deep breath. I try to block out the static of the walkie-talkie, but at the other end Adonis crackles: "How do you get to Staten Island?"

Nigel asks me, "How do you get to Staten Island?"

"You take the ferry. You take a subway all the way downtown. You get off at South Ferry and the ferry is right there. It takes you to Staten Island and it's free and you go right past the Statue of Liberty. You should go."

"Yo, Adonis, we gotta go to Staten Island. We gotta take the ferry. We gotta go—"

"Excuse me!" My hormones trickle all over Nigel. "I don't mean to be rude, but I'm a little antsy today. I've got a lot on my mind. I could really use some quiet."

Nigel does not get defensive. Nigel actually looks a little wounded. "I'm sorry," he says.

Now I am sorry that I said something. "No, no, I'm sorry." After all, the poor guy is just out enjoying the water and the sun. "This is not my personal pier. It is your pier as much as mine, and you were here first."

"No. It's okay. Really. I understand," he says, as if he senses my distress. Maybe the Statue of Liberty's torch has finally hit him with her beam of enlightenment.

"Are you from New Jersey?" I recognize his accent.

Nigel hesitates. New Yorkers are notorious for their disdain of the bridge-and-tunnel crowd. "Yeah . . ."

"It's okay. I just moved to the city. I'm from New Jersey, too."

Nigel brightens. "Oh yeah? Where?"

"Lenape Lakes."

"Never heard of it."

"No one has. Totally white picket. Not far from Paterson."

"Me, I'm from Asbury Park."

"Bruce." I say this low and long, like *Brooooce*. Bruce Springsteen is the Zeus of New Jersey.

"The Man." Nigel grins, and now we are comrades.

Nigel moves away from me, over to where the silver chairs are that nobody ever steals. I am sure everyone thinks about stealing them, the silver chairs and matching little round tables, because they are so nice, but if you carried a chair past a certain point, say, close to West Street, you might get tackled by the passersby, who would protect them. It is something hallowed that they leave chairs out completely liberated in a city like New York, unhampered by chains or bolts, chairs that have achieved liberty and justice for all, and I would like to believe that the passersby would leap to shield their sanctity.

Nigel is still talking to Adonis over by the silver chairs, but I can no longer hear him. I step into the corner spot at the end of the pier where the handrails come together and form a point. I place my hands on either side of the rails. I am the third side of an equilateral triangle. The sun is to my left, a brilliant globe of boiling energy that nobody seems to notice. I think it is strange that there is this thing in the sky that is impossible to look at because it is so bright it will blind you, this thing up there every morning and nobody ever talks about it.

The moon is to my right. Today it is a half-moon, and you can clearly see that the sun is reflecting off this other peculiar object in the sky; there is almost a definite line down the center of the moon where the dark side starts. The silvery moon is another sphere just hanging up there that should be a topic of discussion down here on the planet. It is very apparent that the tug between the sun and the moon is controlling the water today; you can feel the pull and the waves reacting to the magnetic field. Gold and silver; silver and gold. I can feel the sun and the moon inside of *me*, yanking at my fluids. The river gulps and burbles as it strikes the wooden pier; it spits out froth from between the piles supporting the center.

Far away in front of me, I can see the faint glow of the torch of the Statue of Liberty. Her arm is stretched high toward New York City, holding that shining torch like a permanent blessing from the Freemasons in France, just daring the terrorists to knock it out of her grip. Now that I am aligned properly with that flaming torch of reason, I can think.

I feel myself expand. I can get a little more than

halfway across the water today, closer to the Jersey shore. Not bad, considering the circumstances.

I watch the birds fly. Again, I think that it is too strange that we don't talk about this: that there are prehistoric creatures flying through the sky at all hours chortling and screeching and entertaining us with melodies and we never say a word about them. There's a lot of stuff up in the sky that we should be discussing past the age of eight, but only the kids are curious about these topics nowadays; if you try to bring up these subjects, people think you are weird.

I breathe. Relax. Gaze at the water. I go over the scene again in my mind. Even now, I can still feel Evan's sperm entering me from the outside, swimming upstream— rocketing upstream—a mad dash up to my egg, flurries of sperm so desperate to get there that I am almost positive that I am pregnant.

And if I am? *And if I am?* What will I do? I am sixteen and do not wish to be a mother. I wish to be an artist. There is a part of me that loves Evan so much, I wish to have his baby, but there is a pragmatic part that knows it would be disastrous. After all, that's how I landed on earth, when Sean and Peppy, my mother, had their fling. Fling! Tossing love around as if it were a boomerang.

Evan is not a fling, not after two years. But his band is close to a record deal. And I have my exhibition opening tonight over at the Beatrice Snow Gallery in Chelsea.

It has been nine months since I got the call. Certain phone calls are heavy, not cellular, and need the weight of a cord; the memory of this one sucks me off the pier in New York and drops me in the kitchen in New Jersey.

"Harley Columba, please."

"Speaking."

"Hello, Miss Columba. This is Beatrice Snow in New York." The voice sounded like an American with a fake British accent.

At first, I thought it was a friend of my younger brother, Bean, a reptilian creature who delights in practical jokes. "Who?"

"Beatrice Snow. The Beatrice Snow Gallery in Chelsea?" The woman sounded a little offended. "Do you recall sending me some of your work?"

I nearly dropped the phone. "Oh my God! Of course! I thought you were my brother playing a joke."

The voice was not amused. "In any event, you are one of the winners of the Young Artist of the Month competition. Your showing will be in October." I resisted the urge to scream and jump up and down. I started to thank her, but the voice didn't pause. "As I am sure you are aware, in addition to what you already have submitted, I require one new work. That work will then be entered into another competition, along with the eleven other monthly winners. The grand prize will be five thousand dollars cash, plus a showing at my gallery in Venice, in Italy, during their Biennale, all expenses paid. The theme this year is Life Never Stops, in memory of my great friend, Emily Harvey, who is no longer with us."

"I'm sorry," I said automatically.

"If the theme is Life Never Stops, I don't think the words 'I'm sorry' are apropos."

She shrunk me down to a whisper. "I'm sorry." The same words popped out of my mouth. "I mean, I'm sorry that I said I'm sorry." I was making a catastrophe out of the conversation. The image of a girl standing on a mountaintop shouting the words "I'm sorry that I said I'm sorry that I said I'm sorry" forever into the universe flashed in front of my eyes.

To my surprise, Beatrice Snow chuckled. "One could go on eternally with that."

"Right. . . . What are the other requirements?"

"There are no other requirements, except a new work based on that theme. Is that clear?"

She was a drill sergeant and I was a soldier. "Yes, ma'am, it's clear."

"You will receive shipping information with packing and crating directions, together with identification labels. For the Young Artist competition, the gallery absorbs the transportation cost. Thank you for your time. Good-bye."

I stood there holding a dial tone, and then started screaming. . . .

Behind me, I hear a rapid *tap, tap, tap,* a sound that pulls me out of my thoughts and back to the pier. It reminds me of Evan. I turn. Sitting next to a metal lamppost opposite Nigel on his walkie-talkie is a guy with a pair of drumsticks, beating one of those rubber practice circles like the one that Evan always carries around, striking the metal lamppost as a cymbal. So much for silent contemplation; I will be very Zen and accept that today will be a noisy day. I say thank you to the sun and the moon and the Statue of Liberty, and start to jog off back down the pier.

Nigel looks up from his walkie-talkie and waves. "Bye!" he calls.

"Bye!" I wave. "Get a cell phone!" I smile to let him know I am teasing, and Nigel smiles back.

I am going up to the roof. You're not supposed to come up here, because the co-op association says so. I go anyway. This is the notice on the door at the top of the stairs:

YOU ARE TRESPASSING.
VIOLATORS WILL BE PROSECUTED
TO THE FULL EXTENT OF THE LAW.
THIS IS AN EMERGENCY EXIT ONLY.
WHEN ALARM SOUNDS,
POLICE WILL BE CALLED.

I push down hard on the red alarm bar on the door. I brace myself for sirens. Nothing happens. I walk onto the roof, which is covered with cushy asphalt. I have been spying, and I happen to know that the president of the co-op association, Brad Festerly, is up here all the time, smoking and watching the Hudson River. He has the top apartment, and has cluttered the stairway up to the roof with garden supplies and umbrellas, yet he runs around pounding on everyone else's door for breaking the conformity laws if you hang up a skeleton for Halloween. He sorts through all the trash in the recycle bins to make sure you are not mixing paper with plastic, yet leaves his garbage in the hallway at night. If there is one thing that makes me crazy, it is a charlatan.

I have my sketch pad with me; I want to work under the spell of the river in the distance, visible through a gap between the buildings. An enormous weeping willow tree in the backyard of the brownstone next door unfurls its tresses. It is taller than the buildings, living on tree time, not human time, a silent reality check; centuries ago, someone planted it before there were buildings here. The backyard gardens of six brownstones converge below me, three opposite three, forming a brief relief from the on-slaught of surrounding brick and mortar. It's nice up here, and quite stingy of Brad Festerly to keep it to himself.

I flip open my sketch pad and take a piece of charcoal out of its case. I prop the pad on the ledge of the building. I sketch a naked girl into the bark of a tree, arms over her head, submissive, as if she's slid into the trunk from the sky. Her head is tilted toward the sun, and she is singing. I sketch a curled baby inside her belly; it looks like her, but the baby has a flame instead of a tongue. I sketch a preg-nant angel singing down from the sun and touching the girl's song with a stream of octaves, pouring down a wave of musical notes. Inside the angel's belly is a curled baby with a grown-up face, the girl's face; she, too, has a tongue of flame.

This is what I painted in oil for Life Never Stops, my new work for the Emily Harvey competition. I have been working on it for nine months, like growing a baby, long before I thought I was pregnant. I wonder if I painted my-self into the future.

The painting was a long labor and a difficult birth. After the call from Beatrice Snow nine months ago, I stood in the corner of my bedroom in Lenape, staring at the blank white canvas on my easel. It was blank like my brain. I held the sable paintbrush that Granny Harley had bought me, my favorite, my lucky brush. I used to feel her spirit coming through the delicate bristles, the only real thing I could hold on to after she died. I had painted the portrait of Anastasia for the Lenape High School play with that brush, the oil that started me on this path to an art gallery in New York; it had never let me down before.

Anastasia was a Lenape High production, and back then I had the school art room to use as my studio. I had all the supplies I needed, donated by my crinkly fairy godmother, Mrs. Tuttle, whose house I used to clean. But for the Life Never Stops painting, my studio was a corner in my New Jersey bedroom. Mrs. Tuttle had gone abroad, so I was forced to work uptown selling jeans at the Lenape Army & Navy store on the weekends and after school. The conditions were lecherous, but I craved canvas and oil— yellow ochre and rose madder were necessary drugs. I struggled to pay for my own supplies as my fairy godmother faded into a divine memory.

"The theme this year is Life Never Stops." Beatrice Snow's voice echoes in my ears. I can still feel the panic as I faced that canvas in my bedroom. Blank. White. Mocking. Daring me to fill the void. I remember dabbing the brush into a smear of flesh-colored oil paint. I was timid; I thought I would start with something subtle. But when I lifted my brush to the easel, my hand froze and all I felt was fear.

The atmosphere in my house in Lenape was a barrier that blocked access to the part of me that paints. My mother, Peppy, was a constant drizzle. My stepfather, Roger, was a thunderstorm. The only sunshine was my little sister, Lily; my brother, Bean, was more tornado than sibling. It was not possible to work with the weather in that house. Finally, in August, as each day ticked away, I became desperate, so crazy that I worked up my courage and called Sean and asked if I could live in New York with him. After all, he was my real father; we did share the same blood . . . but it was that blank white canvas that forced me to make the call. I had to escape its checkmate; there was no alternative.

Now a voice shatters my memories: "I thought I heard footsteps up here."

I am jolted out of the past and into the present. I turn around to find the voice and look into the sun. I see the silhouette of Brad Festerly, colorless except for his scraggly orange hair poking out from under the rim of a baseball cap, a cigarette dangling from his lips.

"Good morning!" I remind myself that my Life Never Stops painting has been finished; I think it is good; the hard part is past. So I try the friendly approach and offer Brad Festerly a smile inspired by sunshine and the branches of the grand weeping willow tree.

"Good morning? That's all you can say? It is clearly posted that there is no trespassing up here." Brad Festerly exhales through his nose, and he looks like a toxic industrial carrot. "You're the daughter of Sean Shanahan, that weirdo down in 5W, aren't you? I didn't even know he had a kid. What's your name?"

I resist the impulse to defend my father. "Harley."

"Harley, huh? Harley, like the motorcycle?"

I have spent my entire life answering this question and have invented a variety of snappy comebacks, none of which seems appropriate in the present situation. So I say simply: "Exactly."

"You are aware that it's against the rules of the co-op association to come up on the roof, aren't you?"

"I know that you are up here all the time, so I thought the rules didn't really apply. You know? That they weren't serious rules."

Brad Festerly flicks his ashes over the ledge like he wishes it were me who was going over instead. "You've got some mouth, kid. It's no wonder—look at who your father is. Are you aware that I am the president of the co-op association?"

"So that means you enforce the rules but don't pay any attention to them?" The words tumble out of my mouth before I can stop them.

Brad Festerly moves out of the sun and into my face. "You're a smart-ass, kid. I come up here to make sure everything is okay. It's my job."

Now, I have watched this guy for nearly a month, and I know he is not telling the truth. "You come up here to smoke and watch the river because your wife won't let you smoke in the house. I heard her yelling at you."

For a second, I think he really is going to flip me over the ledge. He lowers the volume of his voice to the level of a cartoon villain. "Watch it, kid. I can make your and your father's lives very, very unpleasant. I'm sure he's violating any number of co-op association rules. You don't want to get on my bad side."

Well, I think it's a little late for that. Brad Festerly's frustration with his wife is leaking into my life. I try to appeal to his sense of aesthetics. "Look. All I want to do is look at the river and draw. It's peaceful up here."

"Well, you can't do it. Now get your ass out of here before I call the cops."

I open my mouth to respond, but then decide against it. There is simply no point in trying to reason with a plebeian. I close the cover of my sketch pad. I put my charcoal back in its case. I walk to the fire door, open it, and let the sound of it slamming shut behind me be my reply.

I am in the Rite Aid store at the corner of Charles and Hudson. I am going to buy a home pregnancy test. The store looks different today, not an ordinary pharmacy at all but one stocked with spies and tattlers and customers who can see right through me, everyone watching me, a sixteen-year-old female who might as well have a stomach the size of a pumpkin because they all can sense that I am pregnant. They are pretending to shop, but in reality they are watching to see where I will go, to see which one of the wide selection of convenient home pregnancy tests I will choose.

There is Halloween stuff on sale in the bins in the front, 75 percent off a witch, 50 percent off Frankenstein. All the Halloween candy is marked down, too, and Halloween is still three weeks away. I am sure it is a plot, a Rite Aid plot, to get you to buy the candy early and, unable to resist, eat it all long before Halloween. Then you must buy more when Halloween really arrives, when I'll bet the prices will go up.

I turn down the feminine-hygiene aisle and wonder why there is no aisle devoted entirely to the hygiene of men. No one is there; at least I will have the illusion of privacy, although I am sure there are clerks gathered in the back room watching the monitors and laughing. I'll bet they are back there hollering and pointing at the monitors, mocking the customers' hair, their clothes, their stomachs and noses. There is probably one camera dedicated entirely to the feminine-hygiene aisle, and a bunch of guys are sitting there eating chicken-salad sandwiches and yelling: Hey, Mike! Check out the tits on this one!

I have never really examined the abundance of offerings before. First, there are tampons and pads, pads for every preference: thin maxis, reinforced, super, classic contoured, and regular. Super long, super long with wings, ultra thin, overnight with wings, and the ultimate: super long ultra thin maxi with wings. There are douches in many flavors: shower fresh, medicated, iodine, vinegar, triple cleansing, and spring flowers. I wonder whose idea it was to make a vagina smell like spring flowers. What's next? Autumn leaves? To be certain you are extra sparkly, there is feminine cleansing wash, ultra cleansing wash, foaming wash, vaginal cleansing dissolving film, and, to wipe it all up, feminine cleansing cloths. For the coup de grâce, we have feminine deodorant in spray, powder, towelette, and suppository forms.

Next, there is the female-ailment section: treatments for yeast infections, vaginal itch, urinary tract infections, PMS, menopause, and more. All the products come in a variety of applications: creams, suppositories, liquids, pills, tubes; products for the squeamish who are too afraid of their genitals to touch them; products for the fearless who prefer to go in there bare-handed. There is everything for all your vaginal needs except for home pregnancy tests.

Why do they *do* that? Where would they be shelved? Probably next to the condoms, up by the pharmacist in the humiliate-the-customer section, the section right out in the open full of private, personal products that you must examine under the scrutiny of the entire West Village.

I walk past the light bulbs and the Combat Quick Kill Formula for cockroaches, and up to the pharmacy counter. Sure enough, there are the home pregnancy tests, stacked above the condoms in a separate display on top of the counter, just eye level with the gray-haired pharmacist, who looks a lot like Mr. Gower in *It's a Wonderful Life,* with trembling hands and the floppy face of an aging hound dog.

My first instinct is to leave and go to another part of town. After all, this is New York City, not Lenape Lakes, and I could go to the Upper East Side where no one knows me or, better yet, down to Chinatown or up to Gramercy Park or anywhere else but the West Village. I am overcome by shyness. I pretend I am examining the ovulation kits.

"Can I help you?" The pharmacist peers at me over his reading glasses from the other side of the counter. The display of home pregnancy tests is directly between us. I am certain he knows exactly what I am after and delights in my discomfort. In fact, I'll bet he shelved the pregnancy tests on top of the counter for the specific purpose of rattling the bones of pregnant teenage girls.

"No thank you." I am polite, hoping that will inspire him to get back to the business of drug dispensing. I wonder if there is a government regulation against underage women buying home pregnancy tests, like cigarettes and beer. Next to the ovulation kits are home drug-testing kits, the kind that Peppy once threatened to use on me. Finding out that she had been snooping through my e-mail and hitting me with parental controls is another reason why I had to get out of her sticky clutches and escape to New

York. So I am pre-programmed to be very, very leery of any offer of help from anyone over the age of twenty. "I'm just looking."

The pharmacist pushes his eyeglasses up on his nose. "Are you sure? You seem to be interested in the home pregnancy tests."

"Do I? When I am standing right in front of the ovulation kits?" My voice comes out a little edgy, but, I'm sorry, I think he is deliberately trying to goad me.

"Do you know what an ovulation kit is used for?"

"Um . . . to test when you ovulate?"

"Do you know what ovulation is?'

"Well, of course I do." This is getting ridiculous. To prove my wealth of knowledge on the topic, I add: "It is when the female releases an egg ready for fertilization by the male sperm."

The pharmacist backs down a little. "It's just that young ladies your age are usually more interested in pregnancy tests than the proper time to conceive a child."

I knew it. He has placed those pregnancy tests right in front of him for humiliation purposes. Just because he's not getting any, he's out to save teenagers from the evils of sex. "I'm twenty-five. My husband and I have repeatedly discussed the subject and have decided after long deliberation that we are ready to have a baby."

"You're married?"

"Yes, I am. My husband is a professor at NYU. He's a bit older than me—a May-December romance, as they say." I am enjoying this; I expound on my fabrication. "He teaches comparative politics. We've been trying to conceive for nearly a year, with no results. Hence, the ovulation kit." There is no way I will be able to buy a pregnancy test in this store now, but it is worth it to watch the pharmacist process this information. He frowns and the folds of his face droop past his chin.

"In that case, may I recommend this one?" He reaches over the counter and picks up a pink box. "It has a 90 percent success rate."

I'd better watch it; my overabundance of hormones is making me act a little wacky in the company of men. I must make a speedy getaway before I actually end up plunking down forty dollars for an ovulation kit I don't want. "Thank you, but I think I will take my business someplace where I don't have to pass an oral examination prior to making a purchase."

The pink ovulation kit tumbles out of the pharmacist's hand. He mutters something and tries to pick it up but, instead, knocks over a vial of pills he is in the process of dispensing. Hundreds of little white tablets spill to the floor. All the other Rite Aid customers stop their shopping and look to see the source of the clatter. I try not to smile, then turn and walk past the Chicken of the Sea two-for-one special, past the bottled water and the sunglasses sale, and head out the automatic door.

I am in the Duane Reade pharmacy over on Avenue
of the Americas. It's still the Village, but far enough
away from our apartment that no one will know me.
This time I will be bold. I march straight past the se-
curity guard at the front door, through the cosmetics
aisle, and back to the pharmacy. Behind the counter
are three chic Asian girl pharmacists—apparently
the career to achieve if you are the daughter of a recently arrived immigrant from the East. I am happy
to know that Asian women in this part of town have
wrestled control of pharmaceuticals out of the fists of
aging hound-dog fundamentalists; these three girls
are all done up with red lipstick and clever hair.

I scan the products. They are pricy, up to eigh-
teen dollars for a box that comes with two pregnancy
tests. You pee on a stick and it gives you instant results. For the truly paranoid, there are products that
indicate whether you are pregnant up to five days *before* your period is due. Of course, those cost more.
With all the douching and washing and foaming
and deodorizing and lubricating, you could spend
your entire paycheck simply on taking care of your
vagina.

One product catches my eye: EZ Test. I like the
sound of it because instead of using pink lines or

blue dots to indicate your test results, it clearly states PREGNANT or NOT PREGNANT in the little window on the stick. Thus, I assume, the name "EZ Test." This, too, comes in a box with one or two tests; it even comes in digital. I think it is too strange that they have digitalized a pregnancy test, which I simply must buy. I hand the money to one of the pharmacists, who cashes me out without a sermon and with a smile, and puts the test in a plastic I ♥ NY shopping bag.

"Thanks," I say.

"No problem," she says.

"Hey, Harley!" says a gusty voice behind me.

I jump. Turn. Oh my God. My father, Sean Shanahan, has appeared right next to me in the condom section. My instinct is to hide the bag behind my back, but I resist.

"Sean! What are you doing here?" I try to make my voice sound normal. I call my father "Sean" because I have another father that I call "Dad," whose name outside the house is Roger. Roger lives in New Jersey with Peppy because he is married to her. He is the father of my sister, Lily, and my brother, Bean, but he is not the father of me.

"I'm just buying some condoms. There's an understudy at the theater that I've got my eye on." He winks.

I cringe. That's my dad. It's only been two years since I discovered that Sean Shanahan was my real father, and you can see why they tried to hide this information from me. He also happens to be the father of my ex–best friend, Carla. As far as I know, that is the extent of his children, though I would not be surprised if someone else popped up. Peppy calls him "the cad," and, honestly, she does have a point. Dear Old Dad the Cad impregnated two women simultaneously in the same town and then trotted off to New York City, leaving behind only a crumb with which to find him. Last summer, Carla's mom, Ronnie, finally found out that Sean was not only the father of Carla but also the father of me, and I was the one who was trapped into telling her.

It was just over a year ago and I was in Eternity, this New Age shop that appeared like a spaceship in the center of Lenape. I was buying different stones to balance my chakras, which was all the rage. I loved to talk to Sofia, the owner, the only person in town who seemed to have a clue. She was charming like a cherub, with golden red hair and an angel smile. She was elegant and smart, and always decked out in Armani and Gucci that she found hidden on the racks at outlet stores. She used to be a hospice nurse but wanted a wider audience. Her shop was only five down from the Army & Navy store, so I could escape for a few minutes during my break. I was so starved for conversation that I dumped my whole life onto her shoulders.

"And here is a nice piece of amethyst quartz for your third eye." Sofia handed me a chunk of lavender stone that looked like it came from the moon. That day, she was wearing a gold silk blouse that accented the gold in her hair, and brown slacks. "It's supposed to balance you. Give you more energy."

"Does this really work?"

"Well, I can't give money-back guarantees, but it certainly doesn't hurt." Sofia winked. "What do you want to do?"

"I want to get to know my father," I said. "We basically never see each other. He hardly ever returns my calls. I know he's really busy, but . . ." The stone shimmered in my hand. I heard bells jingle as someone walked in the shop behind me. "He's Sean Shanahan. He's a scenic designer on Broadway. You know the musical *Tall Tales*?"

Sofia nodded. "I went to see it a few months ago. I cried! We all cried. That show was like a thunderstorm that cleared the air. Fantastic. Did he design the sets for that?"

"Yes." I was actually very proud to be the daughter of a famous Broadway set designer, even though he didn't seem to know I existed.

"You're Sean Shanahan's daughter? Didn't he win a Tony for *Tall Tales*?"

"Yes. Yes. He—"

"Harley, *what* did you say?" I felt someone's fingers grab my shoulder and a voice grab my core.

I turned and looked straight into the eyes of Ronnie Van Owen, which were emitting a dazzling array of emotions at the same time. Next to her stood my secret half sister, Carla, shooting daggers and knives. They were next to the Sacred Sounds music rack wearing matching tight jeans and low-cut sweaters, and for a moment, I thought the entire rack was going over. I quickly processed the situation and concluded I was a reluctant messenger about to get shot. "Ronnie, I tried to tell Carla. I really did. She didn't want to hear it."

For a long moment, Ronnie didn't do anything; she just stood there and absorbed the information. Then she spun and faced Carla, who has the same blue eyes as me; the same blue eyes as Sean. There was no denying the evidence. "Is that true? You knew that Sean was Harley's father, too? And you didn't tell me?"

Our blue eyes grew wide and round. Carla shook her

head. "I thought she was crazy. I didn't want to get you all weirded out."

Ronnie turned back to me. "It's not true." She stated this as a fact, as if her words could undo reality, but she looked like she might cry; her words didn't match her face. "It's impossible. That means Peppy . . ." She grabbed my arm and pulled me toward her. "Are you sure? Why do you think Sean is your father?" I don't think she realized it, but her fingers had turned into spikes and they hurt.

"I found a harlequin doll in my storage area. There was a note around its neck that said: 'Papa loves you forever and a day.' " I tugged my arm out of Ronnie's grasp. "It took me a long time, but finally I figured out that Sean wrote the note. So I went to New York City to track him down." Honestly, I didn't think the imparting of this information should be my project; it's not like I had anything to do with their teenage tango. But I remembered my own shock when I found out, and tried to be kind. "I confronted him. First he denied it; then he admitted it was true. But I haven't heard much from him since."

Ronnie's face registered betrayal as if it had happened yesterday, not sixteen years ago. Carla was barely four months older than me; it was as if there were some ancient competition for the same sperm. The three of us stood there not moving, uncertain what to do next.

Behind us, Sofia cleared her throat. She stepped out from behind the counter holding a small decanter. She smiled like she was a wise shepherd and we were her little flock. "Um, anyone want a little Harmony Oil? It's on the house."

Now, in the pharmacy, I nudge Sean, who is whistling and stacking boxes of condoms into a pyramid right in front of the Asian girls. I want to pretend he is a stranger, but it is obvious we are together. You would think that with a father like this, I would be more forthcoming about my predicament, but Sean has already started to display occasional parental-like behavior, and I am cautious. On the other hand, he doesn't seem to feel the need to change his lifestyle, although he has yet to bring a girlfriend home. From the quantity of female voices on the answering machine, I gather there is more than one. I have to say, Sean is gorgeous, even if he is my dad. Today he is dressed in loose black linen unbuttoned to reveal just a touch of chest. He wears his hair like an old-fashioned movie star, longish and swept back, and moves like a man who can dance.

"What time are we going to the exhibit?" I change the subject and discreetly sneak the I ♥ NY shopping bag with the pregnancy test into my purse.

"What exhibit?"

"The John Lennon exhibit over in Soho."

Sean smacks his forehead. "Oh yeah. I forgot. How about three o'clock?"

"Um . . . I thought you said we would go this morning. I have to go out to Lenape this afternoon to get my dress for tonight. Evan's going to drive me back into the city with a couple of friends. I wanted to ask you, is it okay if we come by the theater to see the set?" The opportunity to show off my father makes up for certain distinct character flaws, like forgetfulness. The Broadway stage dwarfs the little proscenium in the high school auditorium in Lenape, where my artwork "stole the show" a couple years ago in that spring production of *Anastasia,* according to the North Jersey *Star-Ledger.* Altogether, I painted three portraits of a princess, which the school bought later and displayed in a window in the main corridor. It was the very first sale of my art. After I found out I won the Young Artist of the Month competition, I took that money out of the bank and bought an outfit for the reception tonight. Sofia brought me to a factory outlet, and we got the most elegant designer black silk dress for less than half price. But in my haste to flee Lenape, I left it in the closet. Maybe forgetfulness runs in the family.

Sean hesitates. "There's a tech rehearsal at six-thirty . . . but it's not the best time to visit. It's pretty boring and everyone's on edge."

"I have to be in Chelsea by eight. Beatrice Snow says all the other galleries have their artist receptions from six o'clock to eight, so she has hers from eight o'clock to ten because hers 'is an *event,* not a reception.' " I say these last words in my best Beatrice Snow fake-English-accent impression.

Sean considers this. "Okay, why not. Sure. Come on by. Come in the stage-door entrance. I'll leave your name. It'll be like Take Your Daughter to Work Day. I'll introduce you to the cast and the rest of the crew. As long as it's just a drop-in, I'm sure it'll be fine. It'll be fun."

I am like a daughter doll for him to play with, a character that stepped out from one of his stage sets and into his life. Looking into his eyes is like looking into a mirror; I see myself when I look at him. Sometimes I catch him staring at me, like he can't quite believe that I exist. I feel the same way; I'm afraid if I blink, he might disappear and

I will wake up in my bed in Lenape, with only the remnants of a dream. "And the John Lennon exhibit?"

Sean glances at his watch. "What are you doing now?"

Why, taking a home pregnancy test, Dad, I want to say. Instead, I say: "Um . . . nothing."

"Let's go now. Let me pick out a pack of condoms and we'll head over."

Now, I can understand that Sean is a single man, but it still feels too weird to be shopping for condoms with my father. I lower my eyes to the colorful assortment in front of me so that he does not see the embarrassment flash across my face. Ah, ha. *Here* is the male equivalent of the feminine-hygiene aisle. Evan is in charge of the condom department; I never knew there were so many choices. Trojan, in typical ancient-warrior style, has apparently conquered the market when it comes to sheathing a man's organ. We have Trojan Ultra Thin, Ultra Ribbed, Extended Pleasure Climax Control, Twisted Pleasure . . . that one sounds interesting . . . Very Sensitive, Her Pleasure spermicidal . . . something about that one reminds me of a praying mantis . . . and Shared Sensation, all in lubricated or nonlubricated form. Another brand named Rough Rider with studs sounds wicked.

Sean grabs a box and examines the back. "You know, sperm is a powerful substance. It should be respected." At first, I think he is reading the words on the box, but then I realize he is voicing his opinion. "A human being can be created from sperm, that's how potent it is." He talks to the box, but I think he is really talking to me. I am startled by his words; can he read my mind? He puts down the box and picks up another. "It's like driving a car. Accidents occur more often when you're young. A condom is choice, and choice is freedom." I feel my face get hot. I cannot believe Sean is giving me a sex-education lesson in the middle of a pharmacy when I, myself, am five days late. To hear the words come out of my father's mouth sounds utterly different than from the mouth of a teacher, who makes the topic of conception seem like a distant subject, like math. "Let's get an optimistic box of thirty." He still is not looking at me, which is a good thing because I am about to collapse on the floor. "I hope the understudy appreciates my selection."

The same pharmacist rings up Sean, which she does with another unbiased smile while I stand there, shaken. Sean rips open the box, takes out three condoms, and sticks them in his wallet. Finally, he looks at me. "Are you stopping at the apartment before you head out to Lenape?"

"I . . . I have to." I stumble over the words. "I . . . um . . . want to get my backpack so I can bring back my dress for tonight."

He hands me the bag with the rest of the condoms. "Can you stick these in your handbag?"

"Um . . . sure." I take the bag from Sean and put it in my purse next to the pregnancy test. I keep my head down so he cannot see how traumatized I am. It's getting a little crowded in there with all these pharmaceutical supplies. Luckily, I always tote around a bag the size of a suitcase; I need my sketch pad and charcoal with me at all times.

"Feel free to help yourself if you need any."

This time I am too shocked to say anything. I look up. Sean smiles, and something about the way he does it makes him look like a knowing parent. Now I am sure that this was all for my benefit, as if somehow he has sensed my predicament and is offering his form of fatherly advice.

"Thank you . . . Sean," I manage to say, and think how different things would be if only he had bought them for me a month before.

"Look how the light hits that window." Sean grabs my arm as we walk along Wooster Street down in Soho. He startles me out of a prayer. I was busy making trade-offs with God: if I am not pregnant, I will join a convent. . . . He points at the top of a building with a marble façade. "Do you see that color? Sort of gold with a dash of blue?"

I glance up. "Yes . . ."

He turns me toward the sun. "Now follow the light up to those clouds. Spokes! Do you see the shafts of light cutting through the clouds?"

He is excited, but I am not getting it. "Uh-huh . . ."

"We had been trying to figure out how to get the stage to look like the hull of a ship, just a hint that the actors are in the bottom of an old boat, without building the whole damn boat. I kept saying we can do it with light . . . the lighting designer was going nuts about it. But that was it: spokes. Just shafts of light, and then maybe some water sounds. So we tried it, and we think it works. We'll see tonight."

Now the scene appears in front of my eyes. "A dark stage with shafts of light like the cracks in the floor of a ship? And the beams move? They rock like the water?"

"Exactly."

"And then some splashing and creaking—"

"You got it. Here we are."

We stop in front of one of those airy Soho spaces, rented just for the Happy Birthday John Lennon exhibit. The line to get inside is a mishmash of humanity, everyone from moon-headed men with silver ponytails to Upper East Side matrons, young rockers to hip executives and their mates. There is even a pair of priests.

"What a mix of people," Sean says.

We take our place at the end of the long line. "And so many," I say.

"What time is your bus?"

"Twelve-thirty."

"You might have to go straight to Port Authority. Forget about stopping at the apartment for the backpack."

"I can just put the dress in a shopping bag or something."

"Or you can stay in the city and buy a new one. I'll give you the money. An opening-night gift from me to you."

"I bought this dress just for tonight with the money the school gave me for my portraits. So it sort of has to be this particular dress." I don't tell him this, but since Evan is driving me back, I was looking forward to the ride. We've both been so busy, me with school and finishing the portrait and Evan with his band, that we haven't seen each other since the moment of conception and I want to talk to him. "Plus, well . . . I did want to get some other things. I still have a lot of stuff in Lenape."

Sean hesitates. "There's not a lot of room in my apartment, Harley. You don't want to bring too much."

His words remind me that our time together is a test, only a test, and I could still end up back in the inferno. I am straddling two worlds, New York City and Lenape Lakes, the first filled with art and music and books; the other with drones and TV and The Parents from Hell. I look away so he does not see my eyes, which have gone all watery. I step on the foot of the girl in front of me, who unfortunately is wearing sandals. She yelps. I mumble: "Sorry."

She turns and glares at me through long straight bangs that cover her eyes like a Lhasa apso puppy without a barrette. She says, "Watch it. I just did my toes." I am not in the mood to quibble, so I let it pass. I take a breath. I wrestle my mind to focus on right here and now, which happens to be standing in line with Sean to see a John Lennon exhibition surrounded by interesting characters, not quivering in my room in the suburbs listening to Peppy and Roger battle it out downstairs. Whatever happens in the future, the times I snatch alone with my father are golden moments to be hoarded and savored again.

When we reach the guy at the entrance, Sean pushes five dollars into the donation jar, and the guy peels off two round stickers with a self-portrait of John Lennon, copyright by Yoko Ono. Underneath are the words INSTANT KARMA. Sean puts his sticker on his lapel. As I slap my sticker on the outside of my handbag, I think: Instant Karma got me good. I want to rewind the Immaculate Conception scene and change it:

"Do you have a rubber?"

"I'll pull out."

"Are you sure?"

"Sure."

Danger. Danger. I should resist, but he is like chocolate. He melts into me. The music changes. An oboe and a violin begin a duet with notes so pure, octaves direct from the sun to the moon.

"No, Evan. Stop." This time, in my mind, I am cautious. *"I'm a little nervous."*

Evan hesitates, and then kisses my lips. "Okay." Slowly he pulls away. "I think there's a condom in my wallet."

I reach across to the drawer of my nightstand and fumble around inside. I hand a foil-wrapped packet to Evan. "A gift from Sean."

Evan looks at the packet and laughs. He opens the condom. "Tell him I said thanks."

" 'Instant Karma's gonna get you.' " Sean's voice brings me back to the reality that Evan and I did not use a condom and I am five days late.

I force my thoughts behind a smile and offer the next line: " 'Gonna knock you off your feet.' " I take his arm to steady myself. We walk up the steps and in the door.

Inside, there are mobs of people jammed around the artwork. Some big guy wearing Lennon eyeglasses and a plastic ID around his neck is running around saying, "Isn't this wonderful? Isn't this wonderful?" I sign my name in the guestbook. Where it says "Address," I automatically start writing Willoby Court in Lenape, catch myself, and put down West Eleventh Street. John Lennon is singing "In My Life" over the loudspeakers about all the places he remembers, and I am softened by the words.

Sean and I get separated almost immediately, so I move from drawing to drawing on my own. There must be about a hundred pictures with clever titles like *He Tried to Face Reality*: John, naked up in the sky, kicked back in a chair on a cloud, a cigarette dangling from his hand, wearing dark glasses to filter the bright yellow sun shining below. Now *there's* someone thinking about the sun.

Hanging on several columns in the center of the room are fanciful drawings that John created for his own son Sean, colorful sketches of witty animals such as *A Turtle Winning by a Hare:* a green turtle racing a pink rabbit. The best is a camel prancing away from a pyramid: *The Camel Dances and Having Danced Moves On.* It is so good that I worry my exhibit tonight is going to be a disaster.

My stomach growls and I am dizzy. I wonder if I am just nervous about tonight or if I am having an attack of morning sickness at an inappropriate moment. I lean against a column and wait for my head to stop spinning.

Over in the corner, I see a sign that says RESTROOMS. I pull myself together and wriggle through the crowd. In the back of the room is a series of erotic sketches of John and Yoko making love that were banned in the sixties. I overhear a white-haired man in a suit and tie say to his wife, "Banning nature is like trying to ban a bee from a flower. You just get stung." His wife smiles and squeezes his hand, and I think they make a cute couple.

I push open the door of the ladies' room. There is a sink and one stall. It's empty. Good. I lock myself inside. I dig around in my handbag for the pregnancy test. My fingers touch the invitation for my exhibit tonight. I pull it out to see the words for the hundredth time.

It is a bright red postcard that is getting bent from all the activity inside my purse. On the front it says: **life never stops. .** with a little signature: **Ben.** Beatrice Snow explained to me it was the artist Ben Vautier who created the phrase. The back of the postcard says:

The 7th Annual Beatrice Snow Gallery
Most Promising Young Artist Competition
Presents

life never stops..
A Memorial for Emily Harvey

MEET THE OCTOBER
YOUNG ARTIST OF THE MONTH

Harley Columba
NEW ART
NEW LIFE
NEW WORKS
It will start on the 9th of October
and last until the 9th of November.

Opening Reception Saturday, October 9th, 8:00–10:00 p.m.

BEATRICE SNOW GALLERY
529 West 24th Street
New York
212-555-8080

It's real. It is real. The words make the whole thing real.
I really am an artist. I really have an exhibit opening
tonight. People will really come to see my work, just like
they are here looking at John Lennon's work. The immen-
sity of it makes me feel like my mind might explode.

My hands tremble as I put the invitation back in my
purse and dig out the pregnancy test. I open the box and
remove the instructions.

I hear the ladies' room door slam open. A pair of trendy sandals appears at the bottom of the stall. Every toe has a different letter embellished on it. One foot says PEACE. The other foot says LOVE!

"Damn!" says a whiny voice with a snob accent. "Are you going to be long in there? It's an emergency."

I am so startled that I drop the instructions. "I just got in here!"

"What are you doing? Reading a book?"

I realize the toes belong to the Lhasa apso puppy, the same girl whose foot I stepped on outside. I think fast. "Actually, I have my period."

"Darling, if you need instructions to stick in a tampon, better practice first at home."

She is one of those Soho art creatures, I am sure, the type that ranges with the herd. Now that I have more energy, I engage the enemy. "Maybe you want to come in here and show me how to do it?"

There is an actual huff. "Huh! Screw you. I'll use the men's room."

The trendy sandals stomp out the door. I pick the instructions up off the floor. The art creature does have a point—a home pregnancy test should actually be taken at home, not at a John Lennon art exhibit. I put the instructions back in the box and the box back in my purse. I pee, flush the toilet, wash my hands, and head out the door.

John Lennon's voice is droning, "Number nine . . . number nine . . . number nine . . ." over and over from "Revolution 9." Across the room, a drawing catches my eye, a huge John Lennon head towering in the sky, gazing down on three tiny bumps on a horizon line. I push through the crowd until I am right in front of the drawing:

At Last He Could See the Mountains. It reminds me of the pier in the sunshine when I want to stretch all the way to the Statue of Liberty and take the torch out of her hand. That would make a good painting, I think. I would call it *Passing the Torch.*

"I know that feeling." Sean has come up behind me. He indicates the drawing. "When the mountains look like molehills. That's me on a good day."

I nod. "Me too."

"And then there are the opposite days. When I don't have the energy to face a crack in the pavement." Sean puts his arm around my shoulder. "Life was a lot easier last year. Winning the Tony really cranked up the pressure."

It is the first time he has revealed this part of himself to me, and I am flattered. "But is it better?"

Sean contemplates this. "Yeah." Together we share a silent moment, gazing at the drawing. "I'm glad you moved in, Harley," he says, as though he sensed my previous distress. He sings: "It's so nice to have a daughter in the house."

I lean my head, shyly, against his shoulder and freeze the moment into a painting entitled *One Small Happy Family.* Then I feel Sean's cell phone vibrate in the pocket of his jacket and the moment melts.

"Sorry, Harley." Sean removes his arm from my shoulder, takes out the phone, and flips it open. "Hello?"

I can hear a female voice on the other end. Probably another girlfriend. I turn to a picture of John and Yoko on either side of a tiny Sean, holding his hands, parents and child, walking through a grassy meadow. That is a family portrait I never had and never will. I try to imagine Evan, a little son, and me, and all I feel is panic.

Sean's voice comes into focus. "Okay. Okay. I will try to get there. But you've got someone there, right? Round the clock? Good. Okay, Mother. Take care. Bye."

Did I hear that right? Mother? Did Sean just say *Mother*?

Sean closes his cell phone. He takes a breath. He looks at me, and then rattles my world. "Well, Harley, how would you like some company on the bus to Lenape?"

We are going up to Port Authority on the "E" sub-way train, which is running on the "A" track. Why, no one knows. Sean is silent, staring straight ahead, thinking deep thoughts. When I asked him why he was coming with me, he was very mysterious and just said, "You'll see."

I am jammed into the center seat of a row of three, a fat white guy plugged into headphones on one side and Sean on the other. Perpendicular to Sean are two black ladies, one in a red sweater and the other in yellow, who have just settled in with lots of packages. They glance at each other as the train zooms past a stop. Through the window, a blur of people on the platform looks after us, surprise on their faces.

The red lady says: "What kind of train is this? I thought we were getting on an 'E' train. We're going to miss our stop."

The yellow one says: "They are always messing with the system. You'd think they'd tell us some-thing."

Right then, a voice crackles over the loudspeaker. We all strain to listen. The voice is mangled and inco-herent, as if the conductor were deliberately speak-ing into a paper bag with a handkerchief over the microphone. After a solid minute of distortion, the voice stops.

The two ladies look at each other in disbelief. The red one says: "You get that?"

Again the train rockets past a station without stopping. I catch another glimpse of the people waiting outside on the platform, looking bewildered and confused. The wheels clack. The horn blows. The car bounces and jerks. Faster. Faster. All the passengers start tossing glances at each other, nervous, as if we are rushing through a wormhole to another dimension.

Now the red lady's voice is alarmed: "The devil is running this train. This is the train to hell. I am getting off this train."

I am getting worried, too. I glance over at Sean, but he is not paying attention. The fat white guy next to me unplugs his ears. Across the aisle, a little boy wearing a Spider-Man T-shirt starts whimpering. His mother's bangles clang as she gathers him into her arms. Everyone is tense now, shifting in their seats.

"Where is the artist? Where is Harley Columba?"

"Oh, didn't you hear? She was a passenger on that subway disaster this morning. The entire train was killed. It's so tragic."

"How terrible! Especially since she won the Emily Harvey Award. Well, at least her work will live on and inspire an entire generation. . . ."

Somewhere to the left of me, near the front of the car, a clear, articulate male voice starts speaking:

"This is an 'E' train running on the express track, making no stops until Forty-second Street. There was a sick passenger on the 'A' train at Franklin Avenue. Therefore, an 'E' train was diverted from its normal route at Canal Street and switched over to the 'A' track."

I turn toward the voice. The two ladies twist in their seats. Standing next to one of the handrails is a tall, thin, elderly man with chiseled cheekbones. I think he is a Native American Indian. He looks as if he is homeless. He continues:

"Once this train reaches Forty-second Street, it will be switched back to its correct track and make all local 'E' train stops. I repeat: this train is an 'E' train running on the express 'A' train track making no stops until Forty-second Street."

The elderly man stops speaking as suddenly as he started, then folds his hands in front of him like he has just finished presenting the Gettysburg Address.

There is a moment of silence. And then the entire subway car bursts into applause. The ladies laugh with relief. The red one says: "Honey, that was *good*."

The elderly man is a wise shaman taking care of our subway tribe. I feel compelled to get out of my seat and make my way over to him, balancing myself as the train bucks and sways. I say: "Thank you."

The elderly man bows his head and accepts the thanks. "I used to work for the MTA. I used to be a conductor. That was a long time ago. I can't sing and I can't dance, but I still got my history."

I reach into my purse and take out my wallet. I hand the man a dollar. "For you."

The elderly man says: "I don't accept charity. I will, however, sell you some double-A batteries."

"That would be great," I say. "I can always use double-A batteries."

We make the exchange. The elderly man says, "No matter what country you are in, you can run it off a double-A. It's good tender in a city like New York." Carefully he puts the dollar bill into a billfold and smiles down at me. Two of his teeth are missing. "You know, miss, this is my music. You breathe it in; you let it out. You gotta inhale. I've been around a long time and I've learned one thing: if all you do is exhale, you got no breath left for yourself."

Now I am convinced he is a sage sent down from the elders to deliver this message to me. Our eyes connect. I smile back at him to let him know I got it and move back to where Sean is sitting.

The train finally starts to slow down as it pulls into Forty-second Street. I touch Sean's shoulder. "Isn't this our stop?"

Sean blinks up at me as if I've woken him from a dream. "Huh? Are we at Port Authority already?"

I smile, a benevolent Madonna after my encounter with the elderly shaman. "It was a fast train."

Sean gets out of his seat and just stands there. The fat white guy with the headphones realizes where we are and jumps out of his seat. People push past us on their way out the door and stampede off the train.

Sean stares down at the floor. "You know, Harley . . . I don't think I'll go."

I am stunned. "What?"

"I don't think this is a good idea."

All the passengers have exited, and now the people waiting on the platform are piling inside.

"Sean. Don't do this. Come on. We have to get off now or we'll miss the bus." I grab his arm and start to pull him. He resists.

"I'm serious, Harley."

I look into his eyes and realize he is, indeed, not joking. I force myself to be calm and appeal to his sense of logic. "At least, let's discuss this out on the platform. You can always get back on the train."

My words penetrate whatever cloud he has disappeared into. I lead my father off the train just as the doors are closing.

We are five minutes away from Lenape Lakes, New Jersey, home to the Cardinal football team, the Cardinal hockey team, the Cardinal marching band— every organization in Lenape has a cardinal as its symbol. There are real cardinal birds in Lenape, flickers of red-armored warriors perched on the branches and whistling through the sky. They remind me of the troubadours, the knights who sang about love. Maybe the Lenape Indians listened to their song back in the days of George Washington, but in all my years in the town, I was the only person I knew who tried to decipher their tune.

The bus driver has just announced that we are stopping at Wanaque Avenue and not going all the way to the old railway station because the street is blocked off. Apparently, it is the one-hundredth anniversary of the incorporation of Lenape, and there is a centennial celebration in the center of town. After the driver announced it, I remembered I knew about it, but life in New York City is distracting me.

"Another obstacle." Sean slumps farther down in his seat. "I knew I shouldn't have come. I can't be late. I should really be early."

I am getting a tad impatient with dear old Dad. This was the conversation on the bus:

"What's wrong?"

"Nothing."

"Something."

"I've got to call Aldo."

"Who's Aldo?"

"My assistant. I've got to make sure he's got every-thing under control. I should really be at the theater tonight. I should really be there *all* night, not running down to Chelsea."

"So call him. You don't have to go to my exhibit, you know."

"I said I would go. So I'm going."

And so on. Now I say: "Tonight is an important night for me, too."

Sean surprises me by agreeing. "You're right. Sorry, Harley. You're probably more nervous than I am. It's just that I haven't been in Lenape since . . . well, I don't remem-ber when. Fourteen years?"

I am amazed. "You haven't seen your mother in four-teen years?"

"Of course I have. But she always loved to come to the city. Not as much since her husband died . . . but she still managed to make it in for lunch every so often."

"When was the last time you saw her?"

"Oh, I don't know. Not so long ago."

Sean delights in being secretive. It is impossible to get information out of the man when he raises the draw-bridge. The more you insist, the more he resists. I ask the question anyway; the question hanging above our heads; the reason, I assume, for the scene on the subway: "Isn't your mother my grandmother?"

Sean does not answer. Then he says, "I suppose she is. . . . I suppose she is. . . ."

The bus pulls over to the side of the road and stops. The driver talks into the intercom. "Okay, folks. End of the line. This is as far as we go unless you are heading to parts north. Have fun at the celebration." He is a stagecoach driver dropping off a load of pioneers.

About half the bus empties out. For a moment, I think Sean is going to refuse to get off, but he follows me out the door and onto the sidewalk. He stands very still and inhales. I stand next to him as the other people pass us by. I hear music off in the distance, happy trumpets and snare drums and xylophones. We are two space aliens mixed in with the pioneers, strange beings just landed from another planet, the Cardinal marching band announcing our arrival in the town square.

Sean shakes his head like he is trying to get water out of his ears, like he is groping for equilibrium. He bounces on his toes, as if the ground beneath his feet makes the town of Lenape Lakes a reality. He looks around. "It's the same. Except maybe . . . didn't there used to be a stop sign there? Where that signal is?"

I turn and look at the stoplight. "They changed that a long time ago. People weren't stopping, just sliding through, so finally they put in a proper light."

"It was probably a good idea." We are silent, taking in the vibes of Lenape. He smiles, but there is mist in his eyes. Then he says, "To be honest, Harley, I've always been afraid of this place. It's why I don't come back. My mother is an angel, but my father was a frustrated man and he took it out on me. He died when I was eleven years old. I used to have nightmares that he wasn't really dead. There are too many shadows. I'm scared I'll never get away again."

It is the first time he has confided these things to me. "Was he . . . physical?"

"Yeah."

"Like Roger?"

"That, I don't know. Let's not get into it."

To my surprise, instead of sympathy, I feel a tinge of resentment. Thanks to Sean abandoning me, I, too, have had nightmares about Roger, only my "father" is very much alive, and Sean and I have never once spoken about it. "But . . ."

Across the road, something catches his eye. He points to a large grassy knoll surrounded by a circular wooden fence, a ring in the center of the road where three streets converge. "Look at that, Harley!"

So much for getting his empathy; I might as well accept that Sean's wall is higher than Humpty Dumpty's and he is too frightened of falling off. I, on the other hand, try to be understanding and I think: he has revealed too much; he must conceal his core. Then I wonder: since when are daughters supposed to be wiser than their fathers? I swallow. I follow his finger. "What?"

"The Circle. The old Circle!" He laughs, and it sounds a little forced. "I used to spend hours playing in that Circle when I was young, pretending I was inside a place where no one could see me, even though I was out in the open with all the people and cars whizzing by."

I am starting to think that my father must have been a very strange child. Maybe he wanted to run away, like me. The Circle is actually kind of a hazardous place to play because it funnels traffic into three different directions. No one is ever sure who has the right-of-way, and there are near misses every day. "Wasn't that a little dangerous? How old were you?"

"Jeez, Harley, I don't remember. Eight? Nine?" Sean grabs my hand. "Come on." He drags me into the street, as if he were running away from a ghost. Luckily, the road is blocked off; otherwise, some housewife in a minivan probably would have nailed us.

We dash across the road and step onto the grassy surface of the Circle. There is an opening in the wooden fence. We hesitate, and then step through it. Inside the fence is an assortment of plaques and monuments. Sean sniffs the air, and then says, like an Indian, "Ancestors."

He tugs me up a flight of stone steps in the center of the Circle until we are standing on a small plateau. I have never actually been inside the Circle before, even though it is the centerpiece of town; nobody ever comes in here except, apparently, Sean. Mounted on a pedestal is a cannon dated 1865; on the ground next to it is a cement triangle with nine concave circles. "That must be a holder for the cannonballs," I say. "Sort of like the thing you stick the balls in when you play pool."

"Exactly," says Sean. He reaches down and touches one of the circles. "Back in the days when you could look your enemy in the eyes."

I wonder if he is still thinking about his father. I know there are times when I would love to blast Roger with a cannonball. Next to the cement triangle, partially buried in the dirt, I see an object flicker in the sun. I pick it up. It is a flat, charcoal-colored stone, again in the shape of a triangle. I spit on it and wipe it off on my jeans. Then I balance it in the center of my palm and watch the sun hit the stone with crackles of light. "Look."

Sean takes the stone out of my hand. "You know what this is?"

I look up at him. "I think it's an arrowhead."

He grins. "Is that cool or what? I used to collect them when I was a kid. I had maybe nine or ten mounted on a board. They're all over town if you look hard enough. From the Lenape Indians. Now you have an amulet."

"Good," I say. "I could use an amulet."

Sean chuckles. "I could use about ten."

We walk down the steps and over to another section of the Circle. Sean stops in front of a stone plaque off to the side that says:

HERE
WHERE IN MARCH 1782
STOOD
WASHINGTON'S HEADQUARTERS

"You know, when you look at all this stuff, it really makes you think," Sean says. "I forgot that Lenape had all this history."

"I used to do housework for this wealthy woman, Mrs. Tuttle, over on Washington Court," I tell him. "There was a house close by that said it was the headquarters for the Continental Army and that George Washington slept there. I guess ol' George really got around. One of my portraits for the exhibition is of George Washington."

I laugh, but when I glance over at Sean, the look on his face stops me. "You . . . you never told me that you used to clean houses."

"What? I had to. I needed the money." I am surprised

he is concerned that his daughter was being treated like Cinderella. "And it wasn't heavy labor; it was stuff like polishing the brass. I liked it, actually. She always had beautiful music playing and was kind to me. I met her just after my Granny Harley died, so she was kind of like a substitute grandmother. She loved art. She donated a lot of supplies so I could do the artwork for the school play. What's wrong with that?"

I watch him consider this. Finally, he says, "It's just that your room is such a mess, I find it hard to believe." I think something else is bothering him, but this time I don't push it. Probably Lenape is dredging up all kinds of memories. After a moment, he changes the subject and softens his voice. "Anyway, do you know about the mutiny? At Federal Hill?"

I actually do know a bit about Federal Hill; Carla and I used to hang out there all the time. Sean doesn't know it because most of my artwork went straight from Lenape to the gallery, but the mutiny inspired the portrait I painted of George Washington. There is a pond on Federal Hill that they say has a bottomless pit. There are secret caves and the ruins of houses along the path on the way up. It takes maybe about an hour to get there from the center of town, a winding journey through trees and bushes and copperhead snakes. "We studied it in local history. They say that the ghosts of the mutineers still haunt Federal Hill. You can hear them moaning. Tonight you'll see the portrait I did of George Washington. I painted the mutineers across his forehead, like he can't ever get them out of his mind."

Sean looks at me as if he is impressed. "That's really good, Harley."

I always turn red when someone compliments me; I don't know why. "Wait until you see it first. Maybe it's not so good."

Sean puts his hands on my shoulders and morphs into what seems to be his father mode. "When you receive a compliment, accept graciously and say 'Thank you.' Don't apologize."

I try this. "Thank you." My voice is meek. It is strange to have him behave like a father, and I feel, suddenly, like crying; I guess it is an automatic reaction to having been disciplined by Roger Columba, the Beast of the Underworld.

"Yeah." Sean smiles and transforms back into dad-the-pal. "Imagine, Harley. Right where we are standing, in this space at another time stood George Washington. There was an inn on this spot called the Yellow Tavern, and Washington made it his headquarters. Horses and Indians and Revolutionary War soldiers moved through this exact place. Can you feel it?"

Sean gets that set-designer glaze on his face. Once, he told me that he likes to visualize places in real life as if they were taking place on the stage, and I think he has faded right into the Yellow Tavern.

I allow myself to drift inside the Yellow Tavern, too, along with Sean and George Washington. I can almost hear the glasses clink and the murmur of men's voices, and it gives me the shivers. I conjure up my painting. It is the same George Washington portrait that hangs in every school, the one that looks like his teeth hurt. Across the slope of his forehead are three soldiers, blindfolded, with wisps of black moans coming out of their mouths. They are the three ringleaders. Two of the soldiers lie dead on their backs. One remains standing; he is the mutineer whose life was spared after the other two were executed. Twelve white doves circle overhead; they are the mutineers who were ordered to shoot their own comrades. They, too, have black moans coming from their beaks. Underneath, I stenciled the title of a book by this poet, Douglas Blazek, which I found in a secondhand bin: *All Gods Must Learn to Kill.* Then I painted a little tear dripping from the corner of George Washington's eye to indicate his sorrow.

"I used to go up to Federal Hill on the night of the full moon and wait for the ghosts." Sean's voice takes me out of the Yellow Tavern and brings me back to the spot where it used to stand within the Circle. "Once, I thought I heard moans, but it could have been the wind."

I blink. "Me and Carla used to go up there all the time, too, but we never heard anything. That's how I got the idea for the portrait." I watch his face to see if he reacts at the mention of my half sister's name, but he just looks away. I think it is a strange coincidence that Carla and I were once best friends. Or, as Sofia at the Eternity shop would say, it's fate.

"We'd better get going," Sean says after a long moment, and I wonder what he is thinking.

A red cardinal flutters to a stop on top of the cannon and starts singing his song. As Sean and I turn to leave the Circle and head to the center of town, I swear I hear a moan.

We are in front of the library. So is the Cardinal marching band. So are the cheerleaders, the football team, the fencing team, the golf team . . . I never knew they existed . . . where do they play? . . . the baseball team, the basketball team . . . gawky giants from Planet Geek . . . the soccer team, the wrestling team . . . the backs of their uniforms proclaim they are the New Jersey State Champions . . . the Lenape Police Department, the Lenape Fire Department, the mayor of Lenape, and every other arm of the Lenape octopus.

Everyone is dressed in his or her official red Cardinal uniform, and we are floating in a sea of crimson. Across the street, up on a platform, the Lenape High School Cable TV staff is recording the entire adventure. Sean and I stand there and gape.

"Oh wow," I say.

"Incredible," says Sean. "All the uniforms are exactly the same as when I was a boy. It's like the whole town is enclosed in a time capsule."

The Cardinal marching band has just played the final note to one of my old favorites, the theme from *2001: A Space Odyssey*, and for a moment, I am wistful for the past. Tubby Marsha Miller, first clarinet, has conquered the space where I used to stand with my oboe. At least I don't have to wear that bizarre military cap anymore. Her tiny eyes squint from behind silver-rimmed glasses, trying to read the music. She looks like a well-fed rodent.

Mr. Michaels, the conductor, lowers his baton and catches my eye.

"Columba? That you?"

Now, Mr. Michaels is not my favorite person, since he demoted me and compelled me to quit the band. What he didn't understand was that my own private mutiny against the injustices of Peppy and Roger was oozing into every aspect of my life, and I was spiraling out of control. It was a little hard to concentrate on musical notes that kept sliding off the score; I couldn't find the right key to my life, let alone a concerto. Instead of wondering why his best musician was losing it, Mr. Michaels went on the attack. Just the sight of him dredges up my final humiliation.

That day, for the first time in my life, I was late to re-hearsal. I didn't want to go in there and play my solo. The night before, Peppy had drained all the music inside me, like a mother who drinks the sap of her young, and I had nothing left to give. When I finally managed to drag myself into the band room, everybody already had their instruments, and they were in the middle of tuning up without me. Marsha Miller, who played first clarinet, second chair, had her cheeks all puffed out and was blowing with this smug look in her tiny eyes, like she was some kind of conquering hero. When the oboe was not there, the best clarinet took its place. I didn't care. I could play the clarinet better than Marsha Miller, but no one else could play the oboe. I was the first clarinet *or* the oboe, depending on the score. Mr. Michaels tapped his baton and raised his arms. Everyone stopped playing. They all looked at me. "Columba, you're late." Mr. Michaels was dressed in a black suit and tie, as if he were about to open at Carnegie Hall.

"So shoot me." The words spilled out of my mouth before I had a chance to stop them.

"*What* did you say?"

I didn't know what had come over me. "Sorry."

Mr. Michaels set down his baton. "I'll do better than shoot you, Columba. I'll demote you. You're now second-chair clarinet and Miller is first. There will be no oboe."

His words stung my face. The rest of the band shifted and tittered. I wanted to burst into tears. Instead, I raised my chin, defiant. "Fine," I said. "I quit." And that was the end of my Lenape musical career.

Mr. Michaels always lived in his own spotlight and thought he was some grand maestro, with the Cardinal marching band his philharmonic. To accentuate the point, he always called everyone by their last name, and now I see he has not changed his system.

"Yes, it's me, *Harley,* Mr. Michaels." I use my first name to throw him a curve. I am happy to have my new secret-daddy weapon along with me on this venture. "May I introduce Sean Shanahan?"

Instead of offering his hand, Mr. Michaels drops his baton. "Sean?" For a moment, I think he is going to kneel before us. Apparently, they already know each other, and I wonder if he is friend or foe. "Sean Shanahan? Where the hell have you been?"

Sean bends down and picks up Mr. Michaels' baton.

He taps Mr. Michaels on each shoulder as if he were a king inducting a knight, and then hands the baton to Mr. Michaels, shifting the balance of power. He says, "Hello, Charlie. Long time no see."

"Good to see you, Sean." Mr. Michaels dwarfs from Leonard Bernstein into the Dormouse and I am amazed. "What are you doing in Lenape? I heard you're a big shot over on Broadway."

"Well, I don't know how big a shot I am, but you got the venue right." Sean grins, and suddenly I see what Mr. Michaels sees: The Man That Got Away. Sean continues, with an edge: "I see you're still here in town."

I swear, Mr. Michaels actually turns redder than the Cardinal marching band. He lowers his head. "Yeah. Well. You know how it is."

Sean decides to be kind. "Actually, I don't. Sometimes I wish I did."

Mr. Michaels stays humble and parries with a validation. "Naw. Trust me. You did the right thing." I am wondering why Mr. Michaels has turned so meek. Then he looks down at the ground and says: "You still mad about that thing in shop class?"

"Mad? Naw. Why should I be mad?" Sean's voice has a bite. "It only took me an entire month to create that cabin scene out of toothpicks. I thought it was hilarious that you deconstructed the whole thing and used the toothpicks to serve olives. Really. You got me good."

I am riveted by the conversation they are having without me. Apparently, they are old foes. I am sly; I step up to bat. "I never told you, Sean, but I used to play the oboe in the band. Right, Mr. Michaels?"

Sean pauses. He sizes up the situation and then tunes into my vibe. He pitches me the ball. "Is that so? No, Harley, you never did tell me. Why did you stop?"

Mr. Michaels shifts back and forth. His voice changes; he goes on defense. He glances first at Sean, then at me. "What exactly is the relationship here?"

I look up at Sean, waiting for his response, but there is none. Apparently, I am still at the plate. Bases loaded, bottom of the ninth. I swing the bat. "It's a father-daughter team." *Bang.* I hit one over the fence and out of the park.

I watch Mr. Michaels process this information. "I see." He is completely out of his league. He looks back to the Cardinal marching band as if it were a pacifier he was longing to suck. "If you'll both excuse me, I have to conduct 'The Stars and Stripes Forever.' "

" 'The Stars and Stripes Forever'?" says Sean. "You know, I never did like that song." Sean has become my shield; apparently, we share a common enemy, two against the horde. "We'd love to stay and listen, Charlie, but we've both got to get back to the city. I've got a tech rehearsal at six-thirty, and my daughter here has got her first art exhibit over in Chelsea tonight."

Sean holds the tension. Mr. Michaels yields and finally looks me in the eyes. "I heard you won the Young Artist of the Month award over at Beatrice Snow's gallery. Congratulations, Harley."

I swear, that is the first time Mr. Michaels has ever called me by my first name. I decide to forgive him; he is not a worthy opponent. "Thanks," I say.

Sean relaxes. He reaches in his pocket, pulls out his wallet, and hands Mr. Michaels his card. "Look me up the next time you're in town, why don't you, Charlie."

Mr. Michaels accepts Sean's card and examines it like it is an invitation to a private ball. He looks up at Sean. "I don't have a card to give you."

"It's okay." Sean extends his hand. Mr. Michaels shakes it. "Still in the same place?"

Mr. Michaels nods. "Same place."

"Then I know just where to find you." Sean takes my hand. "See you around, Charlie."

"See you around, Sean." Mr. Michaels turns toward the members of the Cardinal marching band, who are slouching about, talking among themselves. He raises his baton and yanks them to attention like a puppeteer pulling on the strings. He lowers his baton in one swift move. As Sean and I head up the center of the street, the crimson marionettes explode into song.

"I don't believe it!" Sean stops in front of one of the long rectangular tables filled with wares that line either side of Wanaque Avenue. A lot of the shop-keepers have taken their business outside, but this particular table is stacked with assorted bags of Hal-loween candy. Behind the table stand five little boys in blue, along with a stern, compact, short-haired mother, one of those women who look like they could have gone either way at birth, male or female, and ended up something in between.

Sean touches the table as if he were afraid his hand would go right through it. "Pack 324!" He turns to me, all excited. "It's my old Cub Scout pack. That's my number, I'm sure of it!" The Cub Scouts behind the table are rolling their eyes and snickering at Sean as if he might be slightly mad.

Next to the table of Cub Scouts is another table stacked with Halloween candy and a swarm of little girls dressed in brown. "Wait a second . . ." I have the same reaction as Sean. "It's *my* old Brownie troop 218! How weird is that?" To make things even stranger, when the woman guarding the girls twirls around, she turns out to be none other than Sofia from the New Age Eternity shop, wearing a sleek green jacket. "Sofia!"

"Harley!" Sofia comes out from behind the table.

She gives me a big hug. "I thought you were in New York City."

"I am. I just came back to get the dress we bought for my opening." I am so happy to see her familiar face that I give her another hug.

"Tonight's the night, right?" Sofia strokes my hair like a mother cat tidying a kitten, and I am comforted by the gesture.

I nod. "Yeah. And I'm a nervous wreck." Plus the fact that I am five days late, I want to say, but, of course, I do not mention this part of my dilemma.

Sofia eyes Sean up and down. "Could this be . . . ?"

I give her a warning with my eyes. I don't want to let Sean know that I've been yapping about him all over town. "This is my father, Sean Shanahan."

Sean extends his hand for Sofia to shake, but instead she embraces him with a New Age hug. "I've heard so much about you!" She is all sunbeams and flowers, and I am worried that Sean is going to bolt right out of there.

Sean hugs her back, but he is walls and bridges, and the connection is not complete. "I don't remember selling Halloween stuff when I was a Scout."

Sofia may be soft on the outside, but she has a firm center; Sean's reaction doesn't throw her off. "Actually, you are our inspiration."

Sean is surprised. "Me?"

Sofia nods. "We're raising money to come see your new show on Broadway. After you won the Tony, you became a hero here in Lenape. The hometown boy who made good." Sofia turns to me and takes my hand. "So is Harley. She's a real inspiration to the girls. Proof that they can grow up in a little town and make it in the big city."

She starts singing "New York, New York," and I feel my cheeks turn redder than the crimson marionettes.

"Harley?" I hear a touch of panic underneath Sean's voice. He looks to me for how to respond. I watch him get that overwhelmed look on his face and I see disaster up ahead. Apparently, he has a problem with intense enthusiasm, the same as me. On top of that, he has been in the city for so long, he has forgotten suburban protocol.

"Sofia's got a fantastic shop here in town called Eternity," I explain. "She sells . . . um . . ." I know that Sean is not going to go for crystals and potions. I rattle off a list of relatable goods. "She sells classical music like Bach and Mozart, beeswax candles, American Indian jewelry, books by Carl Jung and Joseph Campbell, um . . . Venetian glass, Turkish ceramics, stuff like that. You know, creative products."

Sean relaxes. "I didn't think a shop like that could exist in Lenape."

Sofia smiles. "Oh, you'd be surprised at all the changes going on around town." She tones down the New Age and cranks up the efficiency. "I'm on the board of the Chamber of Commerce. They say the state has allotted money so we can put cobblestones in the street and old-fashioned lampposts on the sidewalks. There's even talk of getting the Erie-Lackawanna train to stop here again." She runs a hand through her hair. Her fingers are long and elegant, the kind that can hold the bow of a violin. "Do you like trains?"

Sean nods. He is analyzing Sofia, trying to categorize her, but I think he has never seen anything like this before. "I'm all for trains. I use them all the time in Europe."

This is the first time I've heard Sean mention that he

goes abroad. I swear, I know so little about him. "When do you go to Europe?" I ask.

"I have to go sometimes for work," he informs me without taking his eyes off Sofia. "My parents used to bring me there when I was a kid. Part of the secret of my success is that I'm a great thief." He says this to Sofia, not to me. "I steal a lot of ideas from Italy and France." I do believe I am witnessing a chemical reaction, an encounter between Yin and Yang.

Sofia laughs. "Me too. I do a lot of shopping in Italy."

I watch Sean start to fall under Sofia's spell. "Well, it's nice to meet someone else with a passport."

"Likewise. There are some of us even in the suburbs, you know." She tosses her head and her red hair glimmers in the sun.

Sean is actually flustered. "I didn't mean it that way."

"I'll bet I can even beat you to the airport. I fly out of Newark, not JFK."

I don't want to be left out of this conversation. "I have a passport, too. I got it right after Beatrice Snow called me and said I was in the running." I love my passport photo. It took me hours to prepare for it, serious hair and makeup. Since it is valid for ten years, I wanted to be sure my image was captured at its best. "If I win the Emily Harvey competition, I'll get to go to Venice."

Sofia squeezes my hand. "Well, then you must win, Harley. Venice is a great place for artists."

At that moment, a hansom cab passes behind us, a giant white stallion pulling an old-fashioned buggy filled with a family of four. "That looks just like the horse-and-buggies in Central Park," I say.

"That's exactly where it came from," says Sofia. "We

hired it for the celebration. I think it costs ten dollars one way from the library over to the train station. A little touch of New York in Lenape."

Now Sean succumbs completely. He opens his wallet and takes out another business card. He hands it to Sofia. "You know, if your Brownies raise the money, let me know. I think I could at least get you some decent seats and a backstage tour."

Sofia reaches into the pocket of her jacket and fishes out her own business card. It's got a tiny yellow sun snuggled inside a half-moon up in the left-hand corner and ETERNITY in dark gold. "So you don't forget who I am." She hands it to Sean.

Sean grins. "I doubt that."

Sofia turns to me. "Harley, do you have time to say hello to the girls? It would mean a lot to them."

I am touched. I never thought I'd grow up to be a role model for Brownie Scouts. "Sure."

Sean and I walk over to the tables and talk and laugh with the kids. Now that the Scouts know who Sean and I are, they shake our hands and listen like we have wandered out of the Bible bearing stone tablets. We buy a couple small bags of candy to support the cause, and I stick them in my purse. We lose ourselves in their eagerness until Sofia brings us back to reality.

"Shouldn't you two get moving?"

Sean is startled, as if he had forgotten for a moment where he was. He glances at his wrist where a watch is supposed to be, but he has neglected to put it on. "What time is it?"

Sofia's wrists are also bare; she checks her cell phone. "Almost two-thirty."

"Yes. We have to go. Unfortunately." They turn to each other and kiss on both cheeks like they do in Italian movies. "Thank you." Sean doesn't say for what, but it seems appropriate.

Sofia accepts with grace. "You're welcome." She gives me a kiss on both cheeks, too. "Good luck tonight, honey. I'll light a candle for you."

I look deep into Sofia's eyes and see the sun reflect back at me. "Thank you, Sofia." I kiss her one more time. "For everything."

"I should make the trip out to Lenape more often." Sean gets that devilish look in his eye. "There seem to be a lot of improvements over the last fourteen years."

"Sean!" I nudge him in the ribs. "I think she has a boyfriend." We are walking down the center of Wanaque Avenue, which is packed with children eating cotton candy and grown-ups strolling in family units.

Sean waves this off. "Everyone has a boyfriend. If she's not married, there's hope."

"Are those the rules?"

"Those are my rules." Sean says this with a wink but I think he is serious.

I haven't been in the center of town since last June when school got out, and I'm surprised to see that there are several new stores, including a chocolate shop selling bouquets of candy flowers. Maybe Lenape really is making a comeback. We walk past the sewing-machine shop that has been in the same place for as long as I can remember. In the window are evolving models of sewing machines over the years, dating all the way back to an antique black one with a treadle, instead of a motor, that you must push with your feet.

There are three people in front of the shop, a

man, a woman, and a girl about my age. The woman turns and makes eye contact with Sean. She blinks. "Sean?"

Oh. My. God. It is Ronnie Van Owen.

Next to her is my half sister, Carla, Daddy's Other Daughter.

Next to her is a man that I don't know wearing a short-sleeved dress shirt with only the top button open, the round collar of a Fruit-of-the-Loom T-shirt peeking out. The hair on his arms is silver and downy, like delicate steel wool, and I wonder if I could capture the texture on canvas.

Ronnie looks like she might faint right there on the street. *"Sean?"*

I watch the shock on Sean's face turn to surprise and then calm. "Hello, Ronnie. The way things are going, I had a feeling I might bump into you."

Ronnie is motionless, like someone has just shot her with a stun gun. Then she latches on to the short-sleeved man as if he were a life preserver. "Sean, this is Bob McCall, my fiancé." She blusters like she has grabbed the grand prize, but to me, he looks like the consolation. I notice that Ronnie has one of those New Jersey diamonds on her left ring finger, big and gawky, the type you get on sale at Costco. "Bob, this is Sean Shanahan. You know. The man I told you about."

Bob registers this information. The tension in his jaw makes it clear he knows exactly who Sean is. The two men couldn't be more different—Bob with short brown hair tinged with gray, and Sean with long, dark mahogany waves. Sean extends his hand, but Bob doesn't shake it. Bob says, "I can't say I'm pleased to meet you."

Now Carla takes Bob's other arm. Today she is dressed

in Jersey-pink pants with a matching top. Her fingernails are red and look fake. "Bob and Mom are getting married at Christmas," she informs us. Her voice is almost shrill. "We're all going on a cruise together for the honeymoon during the holidays. To the Bahamas."

I try to imagine Sean on a cruise to the Bahamas and nearly start to laugh, but Sean takes it seriously. "Congratulations," he says to the three of them. "I wish you all the best."

"Well, it's more than you ever gave us," Ronnie says, and attempts to turn the scene into a drama.

"Let's not go there." Sean's voice is a friendly suggestion, but underneath there is a warning.

Bob clenches his fists, and for a moment I think he might punch Sean in the face. Ronnie tightens her grip on Bob's arm. I move closer to Sean, who stands there, watching, and does not back down. The power of our unit outweighs the three of them. They seem like part of another species.

I watch the thoughts reel across Bob's face. Sean's not at war here; he's not staking any claim, but he's not backing down from the fight. After a long moment, Bob concedes the skirmish. He relaxes, and then disengages Ronnie's grip from his arm. He extends his hand. "You're right. The past is past." Ronnie is silent but seems disappointed; I think she was hoping for a battle.

Sean shakes Bob's hand. Bob actually seems like he might be a nice guy, even though he's wearing Florsheim shoes.

Then Sean turns to Carla, who is still clinging to Bob's other arm. "You must be Carla."

"That's right." I realize that this is the first time Carla

has ever met her father, my father, our father who art in New York, cursed be thy name. She scowls. "You look exactly like I thought you would."

"I'm not sure whether that's a good or a bad thing."

"It just is."

It is very strange to watch Sean meet Carla; I get a ping of jealousy. The three of us stand next to each other, our blue eyes the only evidence of the relationship. We looked more like sisters before we knew we were related. Carla used to dress like me. Whatever I wore, she wore. Whatever color I painted my nails, hers were the same the next day. Now she has gone to the Dark Side. I would never have fake red fingernails, and I would not be caught dead in Jersey pink. I wouldn't be surprised if next she shows up with a Lhasa apso puppy, complete with barrette.

"You look good, Carla." I take the high road. "Different, but good." This part is true.

Carla gives me the once-over. I am in a low-cut black top and push-up bra, with just a touch of cleavage; jeans; and black, pointy-toe, tiny Italian heels. Evan likes this look; I wear it for him. "You too," she says, and adds a twist: "The same, but good."

"You still with Troy?"

Carla snorts like I have insulted her. "That is so over." She switches into diva mode and tosses her head. "Now I'm with Duncan. He goes to Princeton. Economics major."

I wonder how she met a boy in college, but I don't ask. He's probably a friend of Bob's. "Tonight is my opening at the gallery," I tell her.

"Really? Well, break a leg or whatever it is you artsy types say." Carla looks from Sean to me and something changes. She swallows hard, as if she wants to speak but can't find the words. Then a toad jumps out of her mouth: "It looks like you finally got your wish, Harley. You stole my father." Her voice cracks on the word "father," and I think she is going to cry.

I open my mouth to protest but decide it's better to stand there and take it. I'm afraid if I say anything, I'll start crying, too. Sean speaks up. His voice is soft and kind. "Carla. Don't blame Harley. Blame me. Or don't blame anyone at all, and accept that this is the hand that fate dealt us."

Now silent tears are streaming down Carla's face. "I accept it. But I don't like it." Her tears have touched a place in my heart where our friendship still lives, and I start to cry, too. I want to hug her, but her eyes warn me not to.

"I'm sorry, Carla." Sean touches her hair like a father. "I'm very, very sorry."

For a moment, I think Carla is going to lose it completely and end up sobbing in Sean's arms, but she reaches deep inside and pulls herself together right before the levee breaks. Her voice is tiny: "Okay, okay."

Her running mascara has turned her into a raccoon. Bob hands her a tissue, which she accepts. She blows. He hesitates, and then hands me one, too. "Thanks," I sniff. I blow.

Sean says, "Stop by and see the show if you're ever in New York."

Carla doesn't answer, and neither does Ronnie. Bob does. Apparently, he has become the family spokesman. "We rarely go to New York," Bob says. He puts one arm around Carla and the other around Ronnie, who grinds her head against his shoulder. It is strange to see that Ronnie has conceded her power; she used to be so energetic. "In fact, never. But if you're ever in the market for some life insurance, give me a call."

For a second, I wonder if he is making a joke, and then realize that he actually does sell life insurance. We stand there in awkward silence. Then Sean grins and says, "Life insurance is a perk of my job."

After a beat, Bob grins, too. "With your history, that's lucky for you." The tension breaks, and we all laugh on the edge of crying.

Behind us, there is the sound of a stream of water hitting the pavement. The five of us turn. The white stallion is leaning forward in an awkward position and has stopped to release an enormous flood of urine. Its carriage is surprisingly empty. Sean says, "Now, if you'll excuse us, we have to see a man about a horse." He grabs my hand and lifts me into the carriage, and we click off down Wanaque Avenue.

"The folks before you had a crisis with a baby and a diaper, so I'm empty," the driver calls back to us. "Emergency evacuation. Glad my kids are grown." He wears a black top hat and livery like he is from another century. The Lenape Chamber of Commerce has outdone itself for this centennial; I wonder if it's because Sofia is now on the board. With cobblestones in the road and old-fashioned lampposts, Lenape Lakes could almost become quaint.

"It's our good luck," says Sean. "You arrived at the perfect moment."

Inside my purse, my cell phone starts playing the opening chords to "Ode to Joy" from Beethoven's Ninth Symphony. Nine has always been my favorite number, and I realize that there are a lot of number nines in my life today: it is October 9th. It has been nine months since Beatrice Snow first called me. It takes nine months to make a baby. . . .

I stick my hand inside and feel around the I ♥ NY bags, Halloween candy, and art supplies, and finally dig out the phone. I see it is Evan. "It's Evan," I say to Sean. "Hey!" I say to Evan.

"Hey. Where are you?"

I am so happy to hear his voice I almost drop the phone. "Right this moment, I am in a horse-and-buggy riding down Wanaque Avenue. Sean is with me."

"Sean? Cool. What time do you want me to pick you up?"

"You're never going to believe it, Evan. Guess who we just ran into?"

"Who?"

"Carla and Ronnie and some guy named Bob who says he's marrying Ronnie at Christmas."

"No WAY!"

"It was so intense you cannot believe it. I'm still shaking."

"Look, babe, I can't talk now. We're in the middle of rehearsing and the band is waiting for me. Do you know about what time? Where?"

I speak to Sean. "Evan wants to know what time and where."

Sean thinks. "How far away is he?"

"Evan, how far away are you?"

"About fifteen minutes."

I relay this to Sean.

"Tell him we'll call him when we know, but probably in about an hour."

"Sean says we'll call you when we know, but in about an hour. Is that okay?"

Evan hesitates. "Yeah. Okay. I'll keep the phone by me, but let it ring in case I don't hear it." I hear his bandmate, Oliver, playing a piercing riff on the guitar in the background. Evan hollers to someone. "YEAH! I'M COMING! HANG ON!" He speaks to me. "Look, babe, I gotta go. I'll see you later."

"Okay. Bye, Evan."

"Bye."

I click off the conversation and try to settle back. Now

that I've heard his voice, I am not sure I am ready to face Evan and tell him the news. As the horse-and-buggy clip-clops slowly up Wanaque Avenue, I allow myself to imagine that Evan and I have a baby girl. Seems romantic. Then I watch all the families pass by and realize how far away our stories are from theirs: I have an exhibit opening tonight, Evan is rehearsing with a bunch of black-leather guys, and Sean spends most of his life working in four dimensions. Who is watching the baby?

I wonder if Sean and I are the only space aliens among the earthlings, traveling backward inside our hansom time machine. I turn to Sean. "Why didn't you marry Ronnie?"

Sean is startled. He hesitates, and then decides to answer. "I've told you before, Harley, you were an accident. Carla was a manipulation, a one-night drunken scheme of Ronnie's to get me to come back. I wasn't about to let her trap me into marriage. Even so, I've been sending Ronnie a monthly check for sixteen years now. Not once has she ever said thanks. Instead, she acts like she isn't getting anything."

"Oh." This is news to me. Another piece of the puzzle tumbles into place. I didn't think Ronnie was the type of woman to get pregnant to trap a man, but after seeing that diamond, I can believe it. All this time, I thought Sean was the culprit, but he could have been a casualty. Except . . . drunk or not, with all his talk about the value of sperm, he could have been a little more careful. If you create a human, you must pay for the human, even if you are a space alien. And what about the worth of a womb? I think that would be even more golden. Maybe that's another reason why Sean gave me the condoms, because he doesn't want me to make the same mistakes. Of one thing I am sure: I will not manipulate Evan into having a child. It will be a mutually discussed thing.

"And my mother?"

Sean looks away. "As I've said, I wanted to raise you. I would have married Peppy. But Roger made your mother a better offer. He made me promise not to see you. Your mother and I thought it was best. Peppy wanted to stay in Lenape. I wanted to stay in New York. I was going to art school in the city. . . . That trip back to Lenape through the Lincoln Tunnel was like a voyage from light to dark. It was not a decision I made lightly. We were very young, not much older than you are now. Put yourself in our situation. What would you have done?"

Well, Dad, I am *exactly* in that situation, I want to say, but I don't. Except I am certain that I don't want to live in the darkness of Lenape. Now that we are here, of that I am sure. I just want to get back to the light of New York City and to my exhibition tonight. I suppose I am lucky. I could have been an abortion. Which is the direction where I am starting to lean . . . "I don't know," I respond to Sean. "I really don't know."

The hansom cab passes a group of girls lined up behind two large stereo speakers. A glitzy homemade sign proclaims FUTURE STARS!!! The girl at the mike is singing an old Madonna song, complete with moves, and I see the girls are all from the Joey Barnard Vocal School. I spot the Lenape class nympho, Debbie Nagle, waiting her turn; she sees me at the same time and waves. She shouts, "Hey, Harley, is that you in there?!" She punches the girl next to her, and I see it's her old cohort, Lisa Kowalski. Lisa whistles shrilly through her teeth. "Hey, girl!" They both jump up and down and wave like I am their long-lost cousin, their tiny skirts flying in the air. They are all done up with piles of hair and layers of makeup.

I wave back to them and blow them a kiss. Sean checks them out. "Are those your friends? They look like they like to walk on the wild side."

"Oh, they're okay." I adjust my seat. "I haven't hung out with them for a long time."

"Better that way," he says. "People like that can be distracting." I don't answer, but I know he is right. Debbie and Lisa are part of history.

The hansom cab lumbers past the Army & Navy store where I used to sell jeans. There is a big FOR LEASE sign in the window and a large circular crack in the glass, like the web of a black widow spider. It is an angry exclamation point; someone must have thrown a rock. I wonder if they had been aiming at the bald head of the store manager, Lynn Fleming. I watch the reflection of the hansom cab travel across the window. My face splinters into a hundred fragments when it hits the crack in the glass, and the memory of my last day at work is jolted to the surface. . . .

I had finally worked up my courage to ask for a raise, and I had to speak to Lynn Fleming. He had no hair and was always frowning but had some fantasy that he appealed to teenage girls. His neurosis was probably deep-rooted because his parents had given him a girl's name. Who'd ever heard of a man named Lynn? I took a deep breath and knocked on the door of his office.

"Enter." He said this with a flourish, as if he were lounging on a sofa at the Playboy mansion. In reality, he was sitting in his cubicle on the edge of his desk, thumbing through the latest issue of some men's magazine.

I didn't think; I just blurted out the words. "I don't understand why I am earning minimum wage and all these other people are getting paid more than me."

"I told you, Harley. You are a student. They are not."

"But now it's summer! I work the same hours. I'm doing the same work that they are! It's not fair!"

He looked up from the magazine. "You've got a pretty face when you wear makeup. You should wear it more often." He tried to turn his frown into a smile but it came out like a leer.

I could apply my makeup using the reflection of your bald head, I wanted to say, but I restrained myself. "What does makeup have to do with my salary?"

Lynn Fleming stood up and spanked me lightly on the butt. "Pretty girls earn more money."

"Hey!" I jumped away from him. "Isn't that against the law?"

"There's no one listening but you and me." Something in his voice sounded a little menacing, and I went on alert. "There are plenty of girls your age that would love to have this job. Girls with a *cooperative* attitude."

I was right. He was a pervert. "Good. Find one of them, then." I wondered what Lynn Fleming's wife would say if she knew he was hitting on high school girls.

Then Lynn Fleming became almost sinister; I half expected horns to sprout out of his head. "Are you saying you quit? If you quit, I don't have to pay you unemployment, you know."

"Whatever." I didn't know if he was telling the truth, but I didn't care. Life was too short to spend it folding jeans in the first place, let alone getting drooled on by a manager creep. "What I am saying is that I would like to be paid what's fair."

"Good luck finding another job." He sat back on the edge of his desk and started flipping again through the magazine. I went out on the floor and finished my shift, and then I never went inside the Army & Navy store again.

The driver yanks me back to the present when he pulls on the reins, and I am surprised to see the horse has already arrived at the old railroad station. "This is the end of the line," says the driver. Part of the carriage blocks my view, and for a wild moment, I think he is the Headless Horseman. Then my vision clears, and I see he is just some guy from New York dressed like a character in a Nathaniel Hawthorne story. Sean and I climb out of the hansom cab and stand in front of the train station. The driver tips his hat to us, and another group climbs in. "Ten bucks even though you didn't take it from the start," says the driver.

"That's okay." Sean reaches into his wallet and pulls out a ten. "It was a good ride," he says, and I wonder where his thoughts had taken him.

We stand in front of the red caboose docked in front of the old railway station. This is where the centennial ends; the streets beyond are empty. To get to the House of Columba, we can walk the silent streets or take a shortcut on the railroad tracks.

"Which way do you want to go?" I ask Sean. "By the streets or the tracks?"

Sean grins. "Which way do you think?"

We start off on top of the railroad ties, which force us to walk in an awkward rhythm, two ties, then one, two ties, then one—the spaces between are too far apart and the ties themselves are too close together to walk in a normal pattern. After a few minutes, we get to the trestle that stretches across the river that runs beside the road. "I wonder if freight trains still run on these tracks," Sean muses.

"I think so," I say. "I always get a little nervous when I get to the center of the trestle, wondering if a train will come. I never had to jump into the river, but I know plenty of people who did."

"You're looking at one," Sean says. "When I was a kid, trains came through here all the time. You had to be good to get across. Tony Colucci and I were at it almost every day, playing chicken with the trains. We must have jumped in the river a dozen times."

He grows excited, remembering. "Come on, let's do it. I could use the rush."

I look at him and think how different Sean is from any other father I know. "Okay . . ."

I lead off. The railroad ties are closer together on the trestle, so we can step on every other one. I keep my eyes down and concentrate. Toe to tie. Toe to tie. Below me, the river rushes past. The water level seems lower than usual; I don't know if it's even safe to jump. The thought makes me stumble. Focus, Harley, focus. Toe to tie. Toe to tie. I get a tingle along my spine as I anticipate hearing the *ding, ding, ding* of the signal alerting us a train is coming. We get

to the center, the point of no return. If the signal starts ringing here, the rule is you must jump because you can never make it all the way across in time. The tension builds and propels me forward. I rush to the end of the trestle, looking down at my feet, watching them move rapidly, carefully aiming for the next tie, doing the railway ballet. Sean performs the same dance right behind me. Finally, there is land beneath our feet. "Safe!" we both shout together, and laugh.

"That was great," I say.

"Really gets the heart pumping," Sean says.

We start walking in the odd rhythm of the railroad ties again, side by side, holding a conversation without any words. It is quiet; the only sound is the songs of the birds. Something about the dynamic reminds me of the first time I finally got my nerve up to work in the same room as Sean.

I had been living in New York City for a little more than a week. Sean was at the theater. He had given me permission to set up my easel in a corner of his studio, and finally the idea for Life Never Stops had come pouring out from somewhere deep inside myself and onto the canvas. Every night before I went to bed, I draped a piece of fabric over the canvas so Sean could not see what I was doing; I am very finicky about letting people see my work before it is finished.

But that night, I was so involved with my painting that I didn't hear him come home until he entered the studio and said, "Hi, Harley." I jumped and nearly dropped my brush. I turned. Sean had plopped onto the sofa and picked up his sketch pad. He started drawing like a maniac. "I just want to get this idea onto the page."

Instead of covering up my painting, I turned back to the easel and continued with my strokes. I was in the middle of painting the baby inside the angel's stomach and I didn't want to stop. After a few moments, I grew accustomed to the sound of Sean's sketching; it was like a friendly metronome that accompanied my own strokes. Instead of freezing up the way I did if Peppy or Roger entered the room, I relaxed into his mode, and I never covered up my painting again.

Now, bumping along on the railroad ties, a kid with a bicycle comes right at us from the opposite direction. Boys are so strange, I think. How much fun can it possibly be to ride a bicycle on railroad ties? As the boy gets closer, I see it is my brother, Bean.

"Bean!" I am happy to see him.

"Hey, Harley." Bean screeches to a stop. "Whatcha doin'?" He asks this like he just saw me yesterday, not more than a month ago, and like it is perfectly normal to run into his older sister on the railroad tracks.

"I'm going to stop at the house to pick up my dress for tonight. It's my exhibit."

"Yeah?" Bean is long and skinny, like a string bean, which is what I used to call him; hence the nickname. "Exhibit for what?"

"My art exhibit, dinghead." I introduce Sean to Bean. "This is Bean. He's my brother. This is Sean. He's my father."

"Hello, Bean," says Sean.

"Hey, Sean." Bean scratches his head. He should be wearing a helmet, but he's a rebel that way. He has dark brown eyes, not blue, the mark of Roger as his father. He addresses me like Sean is not there. "Mom and Dad were just talking about him."

"Really? What were they saying?"

Bean shrugs. "I dunno. I wasn't really listening. Something about him being a jerk."

Sean reacts. "Always nice to hear."

"Are they home?"

"Yeah, they're both in there. Lily too." Bean rocks his bike back and forth. "Look, I gotta get going. Earl's waiting for me uptown."

"We just came from there. It's fun."

"Yeah? Okay. See ya."

"See ya."

"Bye, Bean." Sean offers his hand and Bean shakes it. Then he does a wheelie and bumps off over the tracks.

As we get closer to the House of Columba, I want to go farther away. The two wily old manors that guard either side of the entrance to Willoby Court are in cahoots, facing Ringwood Avenue, the main road, all done up in beveled windows and spiral staircases, giving the impression there's history down the block. But turn the corner and surprise! Tract homes. Rows and rows of houses that are all the same, built in the fifties, nesting grounds for a swarm of androids that crawled out of the suburbs, took a look around, and crept back in again. This is where I grew up. I don't know anybody but Sean who made it out of here alive. I am determined that I will, too.

We walk down Willoby Court. I feel very large and out of place, like Alice in Wonderland after she drank too much magic potion. I am outside myself, watching Sean and me on our way to Peppy's house, keeping an eye out for the Big Bad Wolf. My heart is pounding and I am not quite sure why.

We stop in front of a yellow Cape Cod kind of house, the house where I grew up. Sean contemplates the exterior and hesitates. He says, "I'll wait outside. Are you going to be long?" He seems nervous, too.

"In and out," I say. "I'll just grab my dress and use the toilet." I don't tell him this, but finally I'll have the opportunity to take the pregnancy test. "Do you want me to call Evan to pick us up?"

"No." Sean fidgets. "We'll walk to my mother's house. You can call him from there." He, too, seems like a character that has wandered into the wrong movie, a swashbuckler dropped into a soap opera. "Better yet, why don't I meet you somewhere?"

"Where?"

"Jeez, I don't know, Harley. There's got to be a place to grab a cup of coffee."

I consider this. "The only places are uptown, where we just came from, or all the way over on the other side of town."

"Okay." Sean looks trapped. "Why don't I go for a walk around the block? It's Willoby *Court,* right? I'll go for a walk around the court. That should take me about ten minutes. How's that?"

"That's good. Just stay on the sidewalk. It makes a circle and will bring you right back here." The last thing I want is to lose Sean somewhere in the wilds of Lenape.

Sean sets off down the sidewalk like he is following the Yellow Brick Road. I walk up to the front porch. I turn and look back at Sean. He has stopped and is looking back at me. He waves. I wave. I nod encouragement. He nods encouragement, and then he starts walking again. There goes daddy.

I go up the three brick steps and onto the porch. I stare at the closed door. I am unsure what to do. Normally, I would just walk in like I have been doing my entire life, but now I feel more like a stranger without a key and think I should ring the bell. Part of me wants to run after Sean and forget the whole thing.

I decide to ring the bell and walk in at the same time. I press the button and turn the knob of the front door. I stick my head in. "Hello?" I step inside.

Directly in front of me are stairs that lead up to my old room, and for a wild moment, I think about dashing up there unnoticed, grabbing my dress, and zipping right back out again, a phantom daughter who uses the house as a closet. My little sister, Lily, however, stands on the steps and blocks my path, together with our dog, Riley. Lily is dressed like a fairy, complete with wings and a magic wand.

"Harley!" Lily flutters down the stairs. She is wearing a tiny white skirt, a leotard, and tights. There is gold glitter on her wings.

Riley barks. He flies down the stairs, wagging his tail and jumping up on me, behaving as if there is absolutely nothing better in his universe than my arrival. I bend down to pet him, and he licks my cheek. I cherish Riley's kisses. They are slobbery and wet, but filled with love.

I pick Lily up and hug her. She weighs as much as a feather. "Lily!" She kisses me all over my face just like Riley, and I realize how much I've missed both of them.

"I miss you, Harley! I miss you so much!" Lily's voice is high and squeaky. "There's nothing to do around here."

I set her down. "What's with the fairy outfit?" Lily spends most of her time in a world of kaleidoscopes and rainbows, far away from the shadows that surround her in real life; I used to worry that she would float off into Neverland and never return, but now I think she's okay. There have been many times I wanted to go there with her. . . .

Lily spins around and taps me with her magic wand. "I am Joan, the queen of the fairies."

"Joan? What kind of name is 'Joan' for a fairy?"

Lily's face crumples. "It's just my name is all."

I ruffle her hair. "Joan is a perfect name. Where are Mom and Dad?"

"I dunno."

I think fast. If I don't take the pregnancy test before Peppy gets her clutches into me, I'll never have the chance to do it. "I'm going to run upstairs and get my dress. I'll be right down." I take the steps two at a time. I head into my bedroom and stop. The curtains are drawn, and it is cool and dark like a tomb. Everything is exactly as I left it, as if the room were waiting to snatch me back. Lily's bed is straight ahead, blanketed with stuffed animals. My bed is to the left; the covers are aligned perfectly, like a professional maid had carefully arranged the composition. That would be Peppy's artwork. I shudder, and tumble headfirst into the nightmare of a memory.

One night, I was drifting off to sleep during a galactic battle downstairs between Peppy and Roger. Riley was at the bottom of my bed. I was pretending I was listening to singers in an opera by Wagner, not my parents fighting, when I felt a presence beside me. I opened my eyes and blinked into the darkness. A tiny figure stood next to my bed. "God, Lily, you scared me!" I switched on my lamp.

Downstairs, the voices were still snarling. I heard a door slam, then a shout. *"You call this a life?"* I shuddered. One day they would kill each other and that would be the end.

Lily looked like she'd been crying for hours. "Sorry, Harley." Poor kid. I brushed the hair off her face. I lifted up my covers. "Climb into my tent, Pocahontas."

Lily tumbled in next to me. Riley raised his head and yawned. Lily's body was quivering. "You wanna see something cool?" I asked her. Lily nodded her head. "You have to promise not to tell anybody."

She nodded again, very solemnly. "I promise."

"Okay. Close your eyes." Lately I had been sleeping with my harlequin. I knew it was stupid, but he made me feel safe. I pulled him out from under the covers. "Okay, open!"

Lily turned around, and I handed her the doll. She smiled. "Ooo, it's a clown." She cradled the harlequin like a baby. "Where'd you get him?"

"A long time ago, when I was younger than you, my real daddy gave him to me for protection. It's a magic clown. He watches over me with his baton so no one can hurt me. See, it says, 'Papa loves you forever and a day.' Nice, huh?" I clicked off my lamp. I wrapped Lily and the harlequin together in my arms. She weighed as much as a cobweb.

Lily kissed the harlequin. "Will he protect me, too?"

"Protect you from what?" Lily and I jumped. Roger loomed in the doorway. His victory downstairs was not enough to satisfy him. He had tasted blood and come upstairs to conquer the rest of the house. I felt thunder enter the room. I closed my eyes and prayed he was a nightmare. "Down, Riley," said the thunder. The voice was real, not a dream. Riley didn't move. Lily started whimpering. "DOWN, Riley!" I felt Riley jump off the bottom of my bed. His footsteps pattered down the hallway. He collapsed in front of Bean's door.

"Get in your own bed, Lily." Now Roger stood over my bed, swaying.

Lily cried harder and pushed her body tight against mine. "I don't want this daddy, I want my real daddy."

Roger grabbed her by the arm and yanked her out of my bed. "When I say get in your own bed, I mean it."

Lily was sobbing now. "Stop, Daddy, you're hurting me." I wanted to rip his hands off her, but I knew if I tried, I would only make it worse.

Roger tossed Lily in her bed like she was dirty laundry going in a hamper. He stood in the middle of the room, fists clenched, breathing, breathing. He was a thunderstorm turning into a hurricane. "Keep that goddamn dog off the bed." As suddenly as he appeared, he was gone.

I trembled from the aftershock. I took a breath and listened, sniffed the air. The storm had passed, for now. I closed my eyes, wrapped my harlequin in my arms, and listened to Lily weep.

Now I stare into the room where I grew up, my eyes gliding over objects that should offer comfort but only seem ominous. I feel as if this room belongs to another person, not myself. This room belongs to my shadow. I hate to think of Lily alone in this room. I feel guilty, like I have abandoned her. Over in the corner is the empty space where my easel, currently in the corner of Sean's studio, used to stand. I get a chill, as though my shadow self has just entered the room behind me and continues to live this life. I open my dresser and snatch a handful of underwear. I head to my closet and grab my black dress with the price tag still on it and my dressy black spike heels. Then I get the hell out of there.

I go into the bathroom and close the door. Roger took the lock off last year because I was smoking in there; it is part of Peppy's invasion system. I pull down my jeans and sit on the toilet. I dig through my pocketbook and take out one of the I ♥ NY shopping bags. I open the bag. Inside are Sean's condoms. I stick the shopping bag back in my purse and take out the other one. I fish out the box that holds the pregnancy test. EZ Test Digital Pregnancy Test. Over 99% Accurate. Results in Words. I open the box and remove the instructions. I try to read, but my hand is shaking and the words are moving. I grip the instructions with both hands. I read:

"1. Take the test stick out of the airtight packet. Remove the cap." That sounds easy, EZ Test.

"2. Locate the arrows on the test stick and the test holder, and line them up." Okay.

"3. Insert the test stick into the test holder. You should feel it snap into place." Hmm. It says to line up the arrows, then insert the test stick. But how can you line up the arrows before inserting the stick?

"4. Wait for the Start Test symbol to appear in the display window. If the window remains blank, the test stick has been inserted incorrectly." EZ Test is getting a little complicated.

"5. Perform the test." Here we have two options. The first is: "Fill a clean, dry container, such as a glass or plastic cup, with a small amount of urine. For approximately 15 seconds, carefully dip the tip of the absorbent strip into the specimen. OR. Place the tip of the absorbent strip directly into your urine stream (pointing down) for 6–7 seconds. Do not get the test holder too wet."

Well, I think I'll opt for the "test directly in your urine stream" method since there is *no* clean, dry container in the box. You'd think they'd give you one, but no.

"6. After 1–3 minutes, your result will appear in the display window." Okay.

Well, that does not sound too difficult. My hands tremble as I remove the holder from the box. I rip open the wrapping of the test stick and allow the stick to drop into my hand. I insert it into the holder and line up the arrows until I hear a click. The little Start Test symbol lights up. It looks sort of like a miniature EZ Test Pregnancy Test, and I wonder why they didn't write the words START TEST instead of using a symbol, since they are touting words.

Next, I try to take the cap off the test stick, but instead of it coming off, the entire stick comes out of the holder. I put it back in and again try to take off the cap. Once more the entire stick comes out of the holder. My hands are really shaking now. What is wrong with this thing? Maybe digital was not the way to go. I grab the instructions and read step 1 again. "Remove the cap." Oh. I was supposed to take off the cap before I put the stick into the holder. Relax, Harley, will you? Just relax and focus.

I take the test stick out of the test holder and yank at the cap. Okay. Now it's off. There is a strip of felt fabric underneath the cap. I guess that's what you pee on. I take a deep breath and try to relax. I stick the pregnancy test between my legs and try to line it up with where I think my urine will hit. I command myself to pee.

Nothing comes out.

Great. I am so nervous that I can't even pee. I take another breath. I try again. Come on, come on . . . nothing.

I swear, there is nothing worse than wanting to pee and you can't. I stand up and hobble over to the sink, my jeans around my ankles. I turn on the faucet, water music to inspire the bladder. I shuffle back over to the toilet and take a seat.

At that moment, there is a pounding on the door. Peppy opens it and sticks her head in.

"Harley! What are you doing here?"

I jump. "Aaaah!!!" The pregnancy test is in my right hand. I lower my hand so that the toilet is blocking Peppy's view. "Jeez, Mom, you scared me! Can't I even pee in peace?"

Peppy closes the door and hollers from the other side. "I'm sorry, but you could at least give me some warning that you're coming!"

I fumble for the protective cap and put it back over the felt on the end of the stick. "I did! I left a message on the machine!" I yank the stick out of the holder and put it back inside the foil wrapping. My hands are shaking so badly, it takes three tries before I get it in. I shove the test back into the box, put the box in the I ♥ NY shopping bag, and jam the bag back in my purse.

"Your brother must have erased the message. He's always erasing the messages and never telling us who called."

I swear, I haven't been in the house for five minutes and already Peppy is driving me nuts. "CAN YOU JUST GIVE ME A MINUTE SO I CAN PEE?" I shout. "I CAN-NOT PEE IF YOU ARE STANDING THERE YELLING AT ME."

"All right." I hear her move away from the door. "I'll be downstairs."

I wait until her footsteps descend the stairs. And then I start to pee.

I walk into the family room. I put my dress and underwear and the Halloween candy in a used Gucci shopping bag that I found under the kitchen sink; it seemed somehow appropriate. Someone must have given the bag to Peppy, because I doubt she has ever been inside Gucci in her life.

Roger is in his Barcalounger watching a car race, a bottle of beer by his side. I guess it's too early even for Roger to start hitting the vodka.

I don't want to call him "Dad." I don't dare call him "Roger." I don't know what to call him, so I just say, "Hello."

"Why, hello, Harley. Long time no see." Roger turns down the volume just a little, but doesn't get up. "Nice of you to honor us with your presence."

He makes me feel like a casual acquaintance that has dropped by unexpectedly, an annoyance he does not want to deal with. "I came to get my dress for tonight." I indicate the Gucci bag.

"I don't think we'll be able to make it into the city tonight." Peppy has come up alongside me. "Your father has got to work early tomorrow morning."

I think she uses the words "your father" on purpose to dig at me. "On Sunday?" My voice cracks, and I am surprised that I am disappointed. I actually didn't expect them to show up on the most important day of my life, but part of me was hoping.

"People need gas on Sundays, too." Roger takes a swig of beer. "It's a big gas day, Sunday. Not as glamorous as some lines of work, but gas stations make the world go round. It's an important commodity."

I can see what kind of mood Roger is in, and I want to get out of here. Without thinking, I glance out past the dining room and through the front window to see if Sean is waiting outside. Peppy follows my gaze. "What are you looking at?" I swallow, but don't answer. She examines my face and then marches to the living room and peers out the curtains. "Is that who I think it is?" Before I can think of how to stop this, she flings open the front door. "Sean? Sean, is that you?" The next thing I know she is out the door and I am left standing there in front of Roger the Fire-Breathing Dragon.

It takes a moment for Roger to process the situation. Then he jams down the lever on the side of the Barca-lounger and lowers the footrest. He wobbles to his feet. "Doesn't the guy have the guts to come into my house?" He strides through the living room and out the front door.

I follow him and stop at the top of the porch. Outside on the front lawn, Sean, Peppy, and Roger stand in a little circle. Roger is still clutching his beer bottle, and I think he is going to break it with one hand. I hesitate, then walk down the stairs and join them. No one says anything. We all stand there, the current underneath pulsing with venom. It is a rerun of the Bob situation cranked up to the max. Now I can understand why Sean didn't want to come to Lenape today.

"Hello, Roger." Sean does not offer his hand.

"Hello, Sean." If Roger had a gun, I think he'd pull the trigger. "You are not a man of your word." Roger says this as if they were picking up a conversation that happened a few days ago, not more than a decade earlier.

"Fourteen years, Roger." Sean speaks quietly. "I haven't stepped foot in this town for fourteen years. Not even to see my mother."

"Don't try to put that on me, Sean. I asked you not to see Peppy. I asked you not to see Harley. Your mother is on the other side of town. We've all kept our mouths shut about your mother. You could have seen her anytime you wanted to and no one would have ever known."

I watch Sean consider this. "You're right." I am surprised that he concedes the point; Roger seems to intimidate him. And then: "I guess I was afraid to come back before. There is nothing worse than leaving your hometown with a dream and returning with just an attempt." His words are a revelation; I thought he was born confident.

Roger grunts. "I never thought I'd hear you admit to being a coward." Then he starts spitting out sentences. "But now you're a big shot. Now you can play daddy. Me, I stayed here and took it. I accepted responsibility. I didn't run off. I've got a lot of regrets, but at least I'm honest."

"I'm trying to make it up to her," Sean says. They speak about me as if I am not standing right there.

"You want her?" Roger glares at me like I am a rabid dog that got into the house. "You can keep her. It's been nice and quiet around here without her."

It is a blow below the belt, and it knocks the air right out of me. My head starts spinning. A child's song echoes in my ears: "Nobody likes me, everybody hates me, I'm gonna go eat worms." I feel the tears sting my eyes.

At that moment, across the street, Mrs. Perez emerges from her house carrying a bucket and heads over to the Honda parked in her driveway. Moments later, Mr. Perez comes out carrying a bunch of rags. "Did ya hook up the hose?" Mrs. Perez hollers at Mr. Perez. "I told you to hook up the hose."

"Yeah, yeah, yeah." Mr. Perez waddles over to the side of the house and starts unwinding a green hose curled like a serpent in the grass.

"She's just a kid, Roger." Sean's voice sounds far away. I want him to put his arm around me, soothe me, anything, but he seems almost paralyzed by Roger's presence.

I look to my mother. Peppy moves next to Roger. She takes his arm. In my absence from the house, they have become a stronger unit; together their energy feels black. Their language says: you are no longer part of this family. We took you in. We chewed you up. We spit you out. I wonder what exactly I did wrong to receive their wrath, but I think I was merely born.

Alone. I am alone. It is familiar, this feeling, and I am sinking with nobody's hand to grasp. I have three parents right there in front of me, but I am an orphan; I am alone. There is nothing to do but remove myself from the situation; I don't even have to close my eyes. It is strange, but suddenly I hope there is a baby inside me because then I will have someone who loves me.

Roger is still talking. "You want to know the truth, Sean?" He is itching to get down and dirty. "Peppy went out with you to get back at me." He begins a tirade, designed to enlighten Sean. "We started up again when we worked together at the chemical plant. She never told you that she was still sleeping with me. It was a fifty-fifty chance that the kid was mine."

Across the street, I see Mrs. Perez position herself so she has a good view of the scene happening on our front lawn. No one else in our little group seems to care that we are being watched.

Roger pauses to see if his litany has hit its mark, but Sean only looks tired. "That doesn't surprise me, Roger. You two had been going together since . . . when? Since you were fourteen?"

I look at my mother. Peppy is not behaving like a woman who is finally seeing her long-lost love; she seems triumphant, like she has plotted this scene before in her mind and now it is finally coming true.

Roger keeps going. "Peppy came back to me when I started seeing someone else. Rosie McNeal. Nice girl. *Wholesome.*"

Peppy says, "I'm sorry, Sean," but she doesn't sound sorry at all; the words sound punitive, like "vengeance is mine."

Now Sean looks at Peppy as if he is noticing she is there for the first time. "It's okay. It was another life, Peppy. We were barely out of high school. The past is past."

Peppy's mouth drops open; apparently, she was hoping for a different response. It is not the reaction Roger is looking for, either. He has been waiting a lifetime to rip into Sean and he is not going to lose his chance. "We had a fight. Peppy ran off to find you. That's my wife's style, Sean, didn't you know? Play one against the other."

"I left that game a long time ago." Sean looks off into the distance. "You've got to understand. I have a whole other life. It's just a memory to me."

"Turn the water off, will ya?" Mr. Perez yells at Mrs. Perez, who is standing there like she's watching the latest movie, not even bothering to pretend she's not eavesdropping. I wonder if she can hear what we are saying.

"Yeah! All right!" Mrs. Perez shuffles to the faucet and turns off the water without taking her eyes from the scene.

Roger points his thumb at me. "The kid was the bait. And we both bit. Except, I swallowed the hook, the line, *and* the sinker. Hell, you should be glad I don't hit you up for back child support."

Now Sean reacts. "You want me to pay more than I've already paid? You want the cash? You . . ." He doesn't finish his sentence, but there is anger in his eyes.

"Sean, maybe you're not getting it." Roger speaks slowly, as if he is explaining something to a moron he doesn't like. "Peppy got pregnant to get away from her father. I should know; I worked for the guy."

Lily comes twirling out the front door in her fairy costume. She waltzes up to us and taps Roger on the arm with her magic wand. "I have turned you into a frog, Daddy. You must croak."

Roger glares at Lily. "Knock it off, I'm talking here."

Lily's face gets all twisted up, and she looks like she is going to burst into tears. "I'm just playing!"

"Not now, Lily." Peppy turns Lily around and aims her back at the house. "Wait inside."

"Peppy got pregnant to get married and get out of the house." Roger is on a roll; there is no stopping him. I wonder who he is trying to punish, Sean, Peppy, or me.

Probably all of us. "You weren't going to give her what she wanted. I was."

"I want to play outside!" Lily folds her arms and turns herself into an unmovable statue.

"Peppy thought I was the one who was going places, that I would be the one who would buy her nice things." Roger doesn't seem to care that he is speaking in front of a seven-year-old child. I resist the urge to put my hands over Lily's ears. "We all know how much my wife likes nice things." Now he turns on Peppy. "Don't you like nice things, Peppy?"

"Lily, I said get in the house now!" Peppy is almost snarling, but she doesn't let go of Roger's arm. I start to realize that they enjoy the downward spiral they are riding. They are creating their own tornado, sucking along everything in its path.

Lily starts crying and runs up on the porch. She opens the door and lets it slam shut behind her. Mrs. Perez moves onto the sidewalk for a better look.

Roger points at Sean and laughs, but it is a bitter laugh. "Who knew you'd actually make something of yourself. That's the biggest joke. That's a great joke. Good joke on Peppy. You turn out to be a Broadway hotshot and I end up owning a gas station." He is still holding the half-empty bottle of beer. He takes a gulp. He wipes his mouth. He looks at Sean. "Want one?"

Sean shakes his head. "No thanks." He takes a deep breath and then exhales. His jaw clenches, but he doesn't say a word. After a long moment, his posture changes. Roger and Peppy brace themselves as if they are expecting an answering barrage. Instead, Sean takes my hand and pulls me away from the tornado. "No. My daughter and I have got to get going. You have your dress, Harley?" Even though his voice is steady, I can feel the rage in his hand.

I manage to nod. I realize I am still holding the Gucci shopping bag. "Yes." My voice is small.

"Okay, then. Let's go." Sean looks at Roger. Finally, he can't resist a retort. "Have another drink, pal, and go watch TV."

Sean and I turn and start to leave. And then everything changes, suddenly, in slow motion. I hear a smash and feel something wet on my back. Something sharp nicks my wrist. I look down and see that it is bleeding. I am confused; I don't know what has happened. Sean turns and I see fury on his face. I turn. Behind us, Roger's beer bottle lies splintered in the grass. He has thrown it so hard it has shattered into slivers, the froth seeping into the lawn like bubbly magma. Roger's face is twisted, breathing, breathing; he is a furious demon straining against his own chains. Peppy is bent over next to him, her face in her hands.

Sean fights for control. I watch him decide not to smash Roger in the face. Instead, he grabs my hand and hauls me toward the sidewalk. Across the street, Mr. and Mrs. Perez stand there and gape.

As we walk up Willoby Court, neither Sean nor I looks back.

We walk, our bodies heavy with the soot of Peppy and Roger. We are over by the Catholic church, and there is a part of me that wants to dash inside and wash myself off with holy water even though I am not religious.

"Your wrist okay?" Sean asks, and he sounds drained.

"Yes. It was only a nick." This is the truth; I licked my wound clean like a fastidious cat. My heart, however, is another matter. I hesitate, then ask: "All those things Roger said about my mother. Are they true?"

Sean does not look at me. "Harley, I don't want to drag this out. As I said, what's past is past."

"But Sean! You said I was an accident and Carla was a manipulation. It sounds to me like I was a manipulation, too."

"Yeah, it does, doesn't it?" Sean's voice has a bitter edge, and I think Roger's words have hurt him more than he let on. "Sorry, Harley, but the way I deal with people like that is to cut them out of my life."

"People like that? Those are my parents!" My voice quivers, and I think I am going to cry. "It's a little hard to cut them out of my life." I look at Sean, but all I see is a wall where his eyes used to be. Instead of offering comfort, he has retreated inside himself and left me alone on the street. At that moment, the bell in the church tower chimes four times, as if it is beckoning me inside. "I'm going to stop in the church for a minute. I just want to light a candle." I do not wait to hear his reply; instead, I dart up the sidewalk in front of the church and blink away my tears.

I dash up the staircase that sprawls like a billowy skirt around the outside of the church. I push on the huge wooden door. It does not open. I push harder. Nothing. I throw all my weight against it, and a little sob flees from my mouth. It is locked.

"I thought churches were always supposed to be open." Sean has come up behind me. He has lightened his voice.

I do not look at him. "I thought so, too." I push against the door one more time, just to be sure. I feel like giving it a kick, but I restrain myself.

At that moment, a priest in a brown robe comes rushing around the corner. He has long, wavy, golden-brown hair and trendy eyeglasses. As he mounts the steps, I see he is wearing sandals and jeans underneath his habit, and I wonder why we did not have priests like this when I was growing up.

"Hello! Can I help you?" He has an accent—I am not sure from where—and is slender as a branch of a willow tree.

I erase the sadness from my voice and force myself to sound normal. "We just wanted to light a candle. We grew up in this town," I say, as if that entitled us to special perks. "But I've never seen you before."

"I am Father Lorenzo, here from Italy. I am visiting for a short time during your centennial." Father Lorenzo offers his hand, and I see he has long, graceful fingers like Sofia's.

"I'm Harley Columba, and this is my father, Sean Shanahan." I shake his hand and get a shock. "Oh!" I laugh automatically in response.

Father Lorenzo wipes his hands on his robe. "Sorry. Too much electricity today." He shakes Sean's hand. "I was playing, how do you say, 'hooky' at the celebration, so I locked the church. I thought no one would want to visit today, but it seems that I was wrong." He pulls out a key-chain loaded with keys from the pocket of his robe. "In any event, it is not a problem because now I am here and I have the key."

He certainly is different from any priest I have met before. He doesn't look like he's old enough to be a priest. He opens the door and we step inside the foyer. I hear classical music playing. "Where is that music coming from?"

Sean tilts his head. "It's Vivaldi, *The Four Seasons*."

"You like it? It is, how do you say, ambience music. It plays constantly on a loop from the *sistema* I set up in the choir loft. To set the scene for meditation." Father Lorenzo pushes open a stained-glass door, and I remember a time, long ago, when a boy named Johnny Bruno kissed me in the choir loft inside this very church. That boy turned out to be less than zero, but at least my first kiss was something inspired. So many things have changed since then; it is a memory that belongs to my silhouette, not to me.

"*The Four Seasons* is one of my favorite concertos," Sean says.

Father Lorenzo grins. "I brought it from the town where I live, from Venice. I am like a virus, making little changes to the system."

We enter the body of the church. The sun splatters the pews with color as it beams through the stained-glass windows. I say, "You're from Venice? That is too strange."

"Yes, I know."

"No, I mean because I am hoping to win an art competition, and the prize is a trip to Venice." I dip my fingers into the holy water at the entrance and make the sign of the cross. Sean looks uncertain, and then follows my lead.

"*Allora,* then I will see you there."

"I hope."

Father Lorenzo winks. "Say a prayer." He looks from me to Sean as if he is trying to sense our dilemma. "So? Anything in particular I can do for you? A little song? A little dance? A little talk?"

For a moment, I want to break down and confess that we have just come straight out of the inferno, but I decide against it. I am afraid that if I start talking, I will never stop.

"Another time," Sean says. He sounds like he means it. "Unfortunately, today we're on a tight schedule."

"I understand." Behind his glasses, Father Lorenzo's eyes are deep wells with two tiny pinpoints of light. He puts his hands on our shoulders, and again I get a shock. He doesn't remove his hand; instead, he squeezes my shoulder blade and I have an odd sensation. I don't know if it is the music, or the holy water, or the touch of Father Lorenzo, but it's as if something cold inside me catches on fire, like the sun has sparked the moon. I look over at Sean, and I see he has got a strange look on his face, too. Father Lorenzo nudges us forward. "Come. Let us all light a candle together. I can use a good wish also."

We walk up the aisle, an ancient triumvirate. Close to

the altar, on the left, there are several tiers of red candles, none of them lit. A painting of what looks like Mary and a little Jesus is above the candles, but it is a Mary I've never seen before. She looks primeval, like her eyes carry important information. She is holding a small Jesus on her lap; just the tip of her right index finger touches his neck while she supports him with her left hand. Jesus looks like a wise little man, not a baby. "I've never seen this painting before."

"You like it? It is a gift from Venice. It is the *Madonna Nicopeia*, a duplication of the one in our Basilica of San Marco. The icon is coming from Constantinople. The Roman emperors carried it at the front of their army. It means Madonna of Victory. The Crusaders conquered it and brought it to Venice. The story is she was painted by Saint Luke the Evangelist. They say she can perform miracles. I am a little in love with her myself. You can make a prayer."

"Well, I know I certainly could use a miracle." Sean manages a smile. He takes a ten-dollar bill out of his wallet and sticks it in the little collection box under the candles. "That should cover both of us."

I am touched that Sean has bought me a miracle. "Thank you." He is still guarded but nods acknowledgment. I take a wooden stick out of the sand in a container on the side of the altar. "Who has a light?"

Father Lorenzo produces some matches from his pocket. He strikes a match and lights the stick. I think about what to wish. I am torn: to not be pregnant, to win the competition, or to save Peppy's and Roger's souls. I decide to wish to win the competition because even if I am pregnant, if I win the competition, my life will be okay, and the souls of Peppy and Roger are already in hell; better to save my own. I concentrate. I try to look the Madonna in the eyes, but she is gazing off to her right as if she can see something I can't. Victory. I want victory. I touch the flame to the very top-center candle, and then hand the stick to Sean. He lights the candle to the right of mine and hands the stick to Father Lorenzo, who lights the candle to the left.

Father Lorenzo makes the sign of the cross; the two of us follow his lead. I wonder what Sean wished for, but I don't dare ask or it won't come true. Maybe he wished to save his dead father's soul, since he already won the Tony. Then I think, maybe I am not allowed to use a prayer as a wish or I will go to hell. I decide to ask the expert. "Are we allowed to use prayers as wishes?"

Father Lorenzo looks confused. "Sorry?"

"Instead of begging for forgiveness for our sins, or re-membering dead people, are we allowed to light a candle and wish for something we want in the future, as long as it's something good?"

Father Lorenzo smiles. "Absolutely. Those are the best kind of prayers, the ones that are wishes for, how do you say . . . propulsion."

Well, I want to propel myself forever out of Lenape. I only wish I could tuck Lily and Bean under my arms and take them with me. Whenever I think of them alone in the house without me to protect them, it strikes a discordant chord deep inside. "Can I light two more candles?" I ask. "For my sister and my brother?"

"*Ma certo.* Of course." As I use my candle to light two

more, Father Lorenzo says, "I will tell you my favorite prayer, the Lord's Prayer, which I am sure you know, though sometimes I think we should start with 'Our Mother,' not 'Our Father.' " He says this with a grin, but I think he is serious. "You can say it with me, if you like."

Oh no. Father Lorenzo is morphing into a priest right in front of our eyes. He starts reciting the Lord's Prayer, and his accent makes the words sound melodic and graceful. Beautiful as he sounds, I have a severe reaction to anything religious. Churches comfort me because they are quiet, but all the sin and suffering and bloody thorns make me nervous. I know Sean feels the same way. That is why I am amazed that Sean and I join in:

> *Our Father which art in heaven*
> *hallowed be Thy name*
> *Thy kingdom come*
> *Thy will be done on earth as it is in heaven.*
>
> *Give us this day our daily bread*
> *Forgive us our trespasses*
> *as we forgive those who trespass against us*
> *Lead us not into temptation*
> *and deliver us from evil.*

I am ready to say "Amen," but Father Lorenzo keeps going. I hesitate, and then realize he is reciting another version, which, for some reason, I happen to know, and so does Sean:

> *"For Thine is the kingdom*
> *the power*
> *and the glory for ever. Amen."*

The "Amen" resonates through the church at the same time as the last note of the Vivaldi concerto; both sounds vibrate into silence. After a long moment, Sean speaks. "I can't remember the last time I said the Lord's Prayer."

"Why did you stress 'Thy' like that?" I ask. " '*Thy* kingdom come.' And the whole rhythm was different. I never heard anybody say it that way before."

Father Lorenzo tilts his head. "For me, it is a mathematical problem. Divide the Lord's Prayer into three times three. Then, it is because I want to remember that it is not *my* will. It is not *my* kingdom; I am only, how do you say, along for the ride."

Sean scoffs at this. "Are you saying you believe in fate?"

"No, no." Father Lorenzo considers this. "Maybe yes. But not the way you think it." He starts to explain, using his hands. "It is more like there are two streams. Most people are in a big stream, like drops of water, going wherever the *corrente,* the current, takes them. But a few people, only a few, are in a smaller stream. In the smaller stream, you can make the choice which current to ride. Then you are living your fate."

I am intrigued by this idea. "How do you get into the smaller stream?"

"You jump across," Father Lorenzo says. "But it is not so easy. You must make your timing correct when the rapids throw you up into the spray and you are close to the other stream. Everyone hits the rapids but not everyone is so clever or strong to jump. You know, when there is a great passion . . . a death, a love, an accident, an illness . . . these kinds of passions; when you hit some type of rapids, not ordinary life, then you can jump. The water hits the rock and turns into spray and the drops all bounce into the air. Whoopee! But maybe only one flies. All the others go back into the big stream, battered about by life until they die. *Basta. Finito.* Over and done and into the ground they go, food for the moon."

Sean shakes his head. "The Catholic Church certainly has changed its dogma since I was a boy. I've never heard anything like that."

"Oh, this is not the position of the Catholic Church." Father Lorenzo smiles. "I told you I was like a virus." There is a short beep. "Excuse me." Father Lorenzo reaches into the pocket of his robe and pulls out a cell phone. "*Sì?*" He listens, and then speaks rapidly in Italian. Sean and I stand there amazed. Father Lorenzo says, "Okay, okay. *Grazie. Arrivederci.*" He closes his cell phone and turns to us. "Sorry. I'm sorry, but I must take care of some important e-mail before it is too late in Rome." Again he reaches into his robe. "Here is a little souvenir that you can carry." He hands us each a laminated card that says "The Lord's Prayer (*interpreted by Father Lorenzo*)" at the top. Sean sticks his in his wallet and I put mine in my purse. "Please stay as long as you like." Father Lorenzo takes my hand and says, "*Buona fortuna.* Good luck in your competition. I will see you in Venice next year, I'm sure." He turns to Sean. "Blessings. I think you will be okay, *sì?*"

Sean nods his head. "I hope."

Father Lorenzo grins. "Okay, then. *Ciao!*" He heads up toward the altar and disappears behind a curtain, and we are left standing in front of the Madonna of Victory, the five candles flickering a promise for the future.

"Who ever heard of a priest with a cell phone?" We walk up the tree-lined street with roots so old the sidewalk has raised bumps and cracks. "Do you think Father Lorenzo is really a priest? Maybe he tied up the real priest in the basement of the church and stole his clothes and is only posing as a priest but is really an escaped convict from Italy."

"Actually, I think he is a monk."

"I think he is a wizard."

"I think he is a Capuchin monk. They have that very long cowl down the back of their habit." Sean seems as fascinated by our divine encounter as I am. "It's been some kind of day." He stops in front of a big white manor with a porch that circles the house like an apron. "Here we are."

I stare at the house; it is a place I know well. I have been so distracted by our encounter with Father Lorenzo that I haven't been paying attention to where we were walking. We are standing directly in front of number 401 in Washington Hill Estates. A huge oak tree extends its branches like an old friend offering a hug. A wicker swing sways gently on the porch. Thick green moss pads the spaces between the cobblestones winding up to the front steps. "It's impossible," I say.

It is the house of my former employer, Mrs. Tuttle.

I turn to Sean. "This . . . this . . . this is the house that I used to clean. This is the house of the woman I was telling you about."

Sean looks up toward the heavens. "I know. I know. I realized it when you told me over at the Circle."

"But it's impossible. Her name is Tuttle. Your name is Shanahan."

"Mrs. Tuttle is my mother. That's the last name of her second husband. She remarried a few years after my father died. Nice guy. Christopher Tuttle."

My heart is thudding so hard I think it will pop out of my chest. "Mrs. Tuttle is my *grandmother*?"

Sean nods. "It seems to be that way."

They say it is a small world; my world has grown microscopic. It is as if some chess player on high has been moving the pieces until they arrived at this moment. Mrs. Tuttle felt so familiar right from the start, as if our chromosomes knew we were related.

I remember that day perfectly; it is associated with music and smells, and conjures up in color. I was dusting when Mrs. Tuttle came into the living room. "Come sit down, Harley. Take a break." I followed her into the kitchen. "Oh, it's good to have a young woman in the house!"

On the table, she had laid out two cups of tea and cookies, which, she informed me, were "biscuits," like at tea in London. I pulled out a chair as if I lived there. I realized that I felt at home. Comfortable. I sipped my tea and munched on a biscuit. Mrs. Tuttle chatted about her last trip to Paris, and how the whole city lit up at night. She talked about foreign countries like they were right next door, not impossible dreams. I listened, enthralled. I remember wondering if she had hired me to do the housework or just to have someone to talk to.

Now I am finally starting to understand why Sean has been behaving so strangely. I start bouncing on my toes. I get excited. "Come on. Come *on*. Let's go inside. Is she all right? Is she okay? What's wrong with her?"

"Calm down, calm down. She fell and broke her hip. We'll see in a minute what kind of shape she's in." Sean climbs the wooden steps and opens the screen door. I follow behind him.

"Do you have the key? How is she going to open the door?"

"Harley, please. Yes, I have the key, but if you remember, I haven't been here in a very long time." He rings the doorbell. "The housekeeper should be here. My mother said she used to be a nurse in El Salvador."

Sure enough, there are footsteps on the other side of the door and the sound of a deadbolt being unlocked. A black-haired woman dressed in white opens the door. "Hello." She smiles, and I like her right away. "Please, come in." Sean and I step across the threshold, the same entrance I have crossed so many times. "I am Abigail," says the woman. She seems efficient but friendly, with copper skin and laughing eyes. "I am taking care of your mother. She told me you were coming."

I look around. Everything is exactly how it was two years ago: the Oriental rugs and hardwood floors; the plants and trees in every corner. My eyes glisten. "It's just as it was. I met her right after my other grandmother died,

Granny Harley. I even called her 'Granny' by mistake! She always made me feel like this was my home. I was so happy here, so happy."

"Me too." Sean's voice is quiet. He looks around the house. "Maybe miracles do happen. . . ." I wonder if he was expecting the ghost of his father to come charging down the stairs, but instead feels the peace.

"Come, please." Abigail starts walking down the hallway. "Miss Eliza is in her bedroom. This way."

We follow Abigail past the rose-colored wallpaper and the oil paintings, so familiar they seem like long-lost friends. I used to dust their golden frames and imagine the day my own paintings would be highlighted like that, elegant and proud. I see a new painting, an oil, a still life with roses, and note the signature, "Eliza Tuttle," in the bottom right-hand corner. Mrs. Tuttle is an artist, too. I always fantasized that we would paint together; maybe now my dream will come true.

Our footsteps are muffled on the thick Oriental carpet. It is like being inside a fuzzy slipper, snug and safe. We reach the hand-carved oak door, its façade embellished with a forest scene. It is open a crack. Sean knocks gently. "Mother?" His voice is tender; he addresses his mother in an old-fashioned, respectful way.

Inside the room, Mrs. Tuttle calls, "Come in, son." Her voice is strong, not weak, and I am relieved.

"She sounds good," Sean whispers. He grins at me, and I see he had been worried, too. "Why don't you wait out here for a minute and we'll give her a big surprise."

He swings the door open and enters the room. I stand back. I can see sunlight flickering through the white lace curtains. Vases of flowers are scattered all over the antique furniture, brilliant bursts of color that splash life throughout the room. "Get Well" cards fill every available space. There is even a bouquet of balloons dangling from the ceiling. I can't see Mrs. Tuttle from my point of view, but I hear her say, "Sean!"

"Look at you. Look at you," Sean says. He sounds concerned. "What have you done to yourself, Mother?"

Mrs. Tuttle chortles her familiar laugh. "It's nothing, really. You know, when you get to be as old as Egypt things start breaking and need to be repaired. I have a new hip better than the old one. The doctor says I can start walking again in a few weeks. It's really nothing."

"I wouldn't call a broken hip 'nothing.' I would definitely call it something. Why didn't you call me from the hospital? If I hadn't been so busy with the damn show, I would have realized we hadn't spoken in a while."

"What could you have done that I didn't do myself? Abigail was here. She wanted to call you, but I knew you were busy, so I told her not to. I only broke this to get you to come home, you know." Mrs. Tuttle's voice is teasing. "I'm too old to keep making that trip into the city."

Sean mumbles something that I can't understand, then he says: "I have a surprise for you, Mother." My heart is thudding so hard I swear I can see it through my blouse. He pauses for effect, and then says: "Come on in."

I take a deep breath and enter the room. Mrs. Tuttle is sitting up in the huge four-poster bed like a queen, her back supported by half a dozen brightly colored cushions. She blinks, and then says, "Harley?" She reaches over to her nightstand and puts on her glasses. "Harley Columba, is that you? Look at you! You've gotten so big! You've turned into a beautiful young woman! You were very pretty before, but now you're just stunning."

I approach the bed, shyly, and give Mrs. Tuttle a kiss on the cheek. "I don't like to see you like this. I always think of you with a palette in your hand."

"My dear girl, soon you will see me again with a palette. Did you see the enormous oil in the hall? The one with the roses?" I nod. "It took me forever, but I wrestled that still life onto the canvas. At my age! You were my inspiration."

The next thing I know I am crying, I am so touched by her words and the thought that she is really my grandmother. I want to crawl into bed beside her and never get out.

"What? Tears? Why?" Mrs. Tuttle looks concerned.

Sean steps next to the bed. "Mother. I . . . we . . . we have something to tell you."

"You're not about to tell me the doctor has informed you that my leg has gangrene, I hope. You two look so somber."

"Somber? Somber?" Sean sits on the edge of the bed and takes Mrs. Tuttle's hand. "Mother, the way you speak! No, it's nothing 'somber' at all. In fact, quite the opposite."

"What?"

"Guess."

"Guess? Guess?" Mrs. Tuttle looks from me to Sean and ponders the situation. "Okay. I'll play—it keeps the cobwebs out of the brain. First, it is very peculiar that you have arrived with Harley."

"Yes . . ." Sean nods.

"So, why? The last I heard, Harley was living in New York City with her long-lost father. Today the both of you show up at my bedside. Knowing you, Sean, I would imagine that father is you."

Bingo. Sean smiles. "I should know better than to challenge you. You always win."

"Always." Mrs. Tuttle smiles, and she looks exactly like Sean. I can't believe I didn't see the resemblance sooner. "To be honest, I already had my suspicions, so it is not a complete surprise." She pats the side of her bed. "Harley. Come here."

Sean releases Mrs. Tuttle's hand and stands up. "Go on. Sit next to your grandmother."

I watch myself move to the bed as if in a dream. I sink into the feather mattress next to Mrs. Tuttle as gently as I can, careful not to hurt her. Her wrinkled hand reaches for my own. She laces her fingers into mine; her hand is warm and soft. She looks into my eyes, and for the first time I see they are as blue as my own, as blue as Sean's. She says simply: "Granddaughter."

The next thing I know, I am in my grandmother's arms, sobbing, sobbing, crying so hard that I think I will never stop. They are tears of joy, a flood of golden tears that starts to fill the crater in my heart. It takes a long time before I realize that I am saying over and over: "Granny. Granny. Granny."

We have spent the last half hour catching up and crying and hugging each other, a box of tissues now half empty. I completely forgot to call Evan until Sean reminded me; now we wait for his arrival. When I told him to pick me up at Mrs. Tuttle's house, where I used to clean, he said, "Huh?" And I said, "I'll tell you later."

I am so anxious to know if I am pregnant before he gets here that I decide to take the pregnancy test in the bathroom down the hall. I wait for a pause in the conversation, which is mostly Sean hyperbolizing how great Nicholas Raftner is to work with. Finally, he takes a breath and I speak up. "Um, I'm going to use the bathroom. I think I better change my clothes here in case I don't have time later. I want to put on my dress. Okay?"

"Honey, you don't have to ask!" Granny says. Granny no longer seems like Mrs. Tuttle to me; now she seems like only Granny, as if I have been calling her that my whole life, not for a half hour. She is like a mother and dead Granny Harley all rolled into one; she is someone who loves me; she is real, and I want to call her Granny. "Make yourself at home. Use the shower, take a bath, anything you like."

I excuse myself, grab my purse and the Gucci

bag, and leave Sean on the bed telling Granny what Nicholas Raftner means by the title *Answers.* He is saying, "So Dagmar, the female protagonist—Melanie Sumner plays her—she's fantastic—keeps asking Louis, the male protagonist, 'Why?' Why this? Why that? Why, why, why . . ."

Their voices fade as I move quickly down the hall, past the oil paintings and the wicker baskets filled with plants. I pause. The signature on an old landscape, a meadow glistening with sunlight, catches my eye: Elizabeth de Berkeley. It looks like Granny's style, but raw and inexperienced, and I wonder if that is Granny's maiden name.

I hear Abigail banging pots and pans in the kitchen, cooking up something for Granny's dinner. Good. The coast is clear. I turn left and let myself into the guest bathroom, which, unlike the House of Columba, has a door that locks. It is small but elegant, with an antique marble sink and a white marble bathtub. The faucets are brass; the towels are plush maroon. I think how much nicer this bathroom is than the one at my house—my former house—and pray that I will never have to go back there again.

Again, I pull down my jeans and sit on the toilet. I take out the pregnancy test. This time I force myself to be efficient and not work myself up into a frenzy, just proceed logically and calmly. I remove the cap. I pop the test stick into the test holder until it clicks; the Start Test symbol appears in the little window. I am matter-of-fact, composed; my hands do not shake at all. I place the pregnancy test between my legs. I start to pee immediately. I count:

one . . . two . . . three . . . four . . . five . . . six . . . seven. . . . I add an eight . . . nine . . . ten . . . just to be safe. I pull the stick away from my stream of urine until I finish peeing. I reach for the toilet paper and tear off a few squares.

And then I lose my grip and drop the super duper EZ Test Digital Pregnancy Test Stick straight into the toilet.

"Oh no!" I gasp. "Oh NO!" I sit there, frozen, unsure what to do. Then I plunge my hand into the toilet and pull out the stick. I remember the words on the instructions: "Do not get the test holder too wet." Well, it doesn't get much wetter than this. I throw the test into the sink. I watch the Start Test symbol disappear. The little window goes blank.

I wipe myself and flush. I pull off my jeans and stand there in my thong. I stare at the pregnancy test and pray. The window is still wordless. Hoping against everything, I wait for the words to appear: PREGNANT or NOT PREGNANT. Nothing happens. I half expect the EZ Test Digital Pregnancy Test to flash back the word IDIOT.

I grab the instructions and read. I skip to Part 6. "If your result does not appear after 3 minutes, please refer to #21 under Frequently Asked Questions."

I flip the instructions over to the Frequently Asked Questions. I skim down to number 21. *"The display window gives no result—it remains blank. What does this mean?* An error has occurred. Please contact our Help Line. *Do not* use this test holder with any remaining test sticks."

I want to cry, I am so frustrated. There is nothing to do but buy another one. I rinse the pregnancy test off and stick it back into the box. I wash my hands twice. I stick the box back into the I ♥ NY shopping bag and put the shopping bag back in my purse. I have to get rid of that thing, but not here.

I decide to take Granny up on her offer and turn on the shower. I feel so grimy that I want to wash myself off before I put on my dress. I take a quick shower, careful not to get my hair wet. I wash between my legs, hoping for a drop of blood, but there is nothing.

The doorbell rings. I turn off the shower and grab a towel. I listen to someone walk into the living room to open the door, and then I hear Evan talking to Abigail. I don't want to leave him out there all alone. I chew the price tag off my new black dress and slip the dress over my head. I fold my clothes into the Gucci shopping bag with the Halloween candy and grab my purse. I slip on my dressy spikes. I check myself out in the mirror. I have to say, the dress has transformed me from rocker to refined. I'll put my makeup on in the car.

I unlock the door and hurry down the hallway, nearly tripping over a bust of Beethoven; spike heels are not the most practical method of transportation. I round the corner and spot Evan standing in the foyer chatting with Abigail about the situation in El Salvador. "Evan!"

"Harley!" He takes in my outfit. "Wow. You look fantastic. You're like an entirely different girl."

"Evan, I am so, so glad to see you." He is wearing his best jeans and a long, black, dressy jacket and black leather boots. The outfit contrasts perfectly with his long blond hair, which is pulled back into a ponytail. He is completely gorgeous. "You look fantastic, too."

I kiss him on the lips, right in front of Abigail. She

blushes. "I will leave you two alone." She heads off into the kitchen.

"No, no, that's okay," I say to her back, but she doesn't stop walking. "I want Granny to meet Evan." I take his hand and start to tug him through the living room.

"Granny? Who's Granny?" Evan allows me to pull him; he looks amused.

I fill him in as quickly as I can on all the events of the day: meeting Carla and Ronnie and Bob, then Sofia, and then the Peppy and Roger extravaganza. Now that he is here with me in this cozy house, the house of my family, Peppy and Roger have faded from black to gray.

We start down the hall. Evan is listening but he seems distracted. I say, "And then Sean—"

Evan stops abruptly beneath an oil painting of Cupid. "Wait."

"What?" I wonder what he is up to, until I catch the look in his eye.

He pulls me toward him and wraps my arm behind my back. "Come here, you." He kisses me. His lips are hard against mine. We haven't seen each other for a month and our kisses are hungry. "You smell good."

"I just took a shower."

"Really?" Evan starts to lift up my skirt.

I grab his wrist. I whisper, "What are you doing?" I am teasing but serious.

"Oh, nothing." He kisses me again. He touches me again. "Those heels are turning me on."

First I think, no, no, no, Evan, I can't, I think I'm pregnant, but he keeps it up and I cannot resist him. I haven't seen him for so long. He is too beautiful; his arms are too safe; his touch is too familiar. Our tongues wrap around each other like two dancing serpents; his hands run up and down my body. After a long moment, we pull apart, breathless. We look in each other's eyes and exchange thoughts.

"Where?" he says.

I think. "The bathroom. Down the hall." I pull him toward the little bathroom on the left. We go inside and lock the door. I set down my purse and the shopping bag. We fall into each other's arms and kiss. "Oh." I tug the elastic off his ponytail and run my fingers through his hair.

Evan cups my breast. "You feel big," he whispers. "Are you getting your period?"

What? His words are a shock and I pull away. "Wait . . ." I remove his hands from my body. "This is not a good idea, Evan. We'd better . . ." My voice cracks. I swallow. "We'd better get going." I look down so he cannot see my eyes. I want to blurt out the truth right there in the bathroom, but this is not the time.

Evan touches my shoulder. He sounds puzzled. "What? What did I say?"

I move away from him and over to the sink. "Nothing . . ." I turn on the faucet and start splashing cold water over my face. I command my mind to be rational: I don't *know* that I am pregnant. I will buy a new pregnancy test tomorrow and take the test in New York City, alone, quiet, private. There is no point in telling Evan about it now. Right now, it is only a worry, not a reality. I grab a towel and pat my face dry; I pat away my fears. I speak into the towel. "It's just that this is my grandmother's house, is all. It doesn't feel right."

Evan hesitates, and then accepts this explanation. He says, "Sorry, babe. You're right. It's just that you look so good, you're hard to resist."

I come out from under the towel. I hang it up on the rack. I glance at myself in the mirror. Except for a trace of worry left in my eyes, I think I look okay. I finally look at Evan. I manage a smile. "Let's meet Granny."

We walk down the hall. Evan has his arm around me. I continue with my story about the trials of today, casually, as if there had been no bathroom interlude. Every time I think the word "pregnancy," I force myself to think: you will buy the test tomorrow, until the thought transforms from worry to reason. We approach the bedroom door just as I am telling Evan the details about Mrs. Tuttle being my grandmother. He shakes his head. "This all happened in *one day*?"

I can even giggle now; I think I could make a good actress. "I know. I know. And we still have to go to my exhibit. I'm exhausted just thinking about it. Here we are."

We stop in front of the hand-carved door, and I give Evan a quick peck on the cheek for encouragement, though he is much better than I am about meeting grown-ups. He enters the room with me and I make the introductions. Even though he's picked me up from this house many times, he never has actually met Mrs. Tut—Granny. We approach the bed. Granny takes in my dress. "Harley, you look enchanting. Very sophisticated."

"Thanks, Granny." I blush. "This is my boyfriend, Evan. Evan, this is my grandmother."

Evan reaches for Granny's outstretched hand and gently shakes it. "Very pleased to meet you, ma'am," he says. Evan has this born ability to make corny things seem natural; I have yet to meet an older woman who doesn't fall for his charm. Now that I see him in action, I think he reminds me a little bit of Sean.

Granny is delighted with her greeting. "Such a polite boy! Please forgive me if I don't get up, but I'm a little incapacitated today."

"A temporary situation, I'm sure." Evan grins, and Granny laps it up.

"Don't you think we should get going?" Sean interrupts the moment, and I get the feeling he might be a little bit jealous; maybe Evan reminds him of a younger version of himself, too. "I can't be late for the tech rehearsal, and there could be a lot of traffic on Saturday night. I have to stop by the theater before we go to the exhibit. I need to see Aldo." Sean treats Evan differently here in Granny's bedroom. He morphs into a proper father, not a pal, now that he is standing in front of Granny.

Evan nods, picking up on Sean's vibe. "Oliver and Jessie are waiting for us out in the car."

Abigail appears in the doorway. "Dinner is ready whenever you are, Miss Eliza."

Granny adjusts her pillows. "Now is fine, Abigail." She looks at the three of us. "As much as I would like to keep you all here with me, I must eat if these old bones are going to heal. Come, give your Granny a kiss good-bye."

I kiss her on the cheek as if I have been doing it for years. "Bye, Granny."

Granny takes both my hands. "Have fun tonight. I'm sure you'll win."

My stomach does a little spin at her words, and I get a

panicky feeling just thinking about the exhibition. "They don't announce the winner until January."

"Only three months to wait, then, before the good news." Granny says this with such confidence that I almost believe her. And at that moment, with all four of us together, I allow myself to think that everything is going to be okay.

We are in Evan's gleaming spacemobile, his blue Camaro with white leather seats that he keeps primed to the max. Sean sits up front next to Evan. I sit on the center hump in the back, wedged in between Oliver and Jessie, because I am the smallest. Oliver and Jessie are my and Evan's best friends. We are four slices that make up a little circle. Jessie was kind to me from the first night I met her at a party at Oliver's house, and now we are The Girlfriends together, which is a status thing when you are traveling with the band. Sometimes it is fun, but lately I get weary. As Evan steers the car out of Lenape, I think about the last time we were at a club with the boys.

It was a place called Hades somewhere in South Jersey. Evan's gigs blur into each other; he is always changing venues. Hades was a warehouse with a dance floor in front and lots of tables in back. There was a fake stream called the River Styx that surrounded the club. The audience had to pay first to cross over the bridge that led inside, just like crossing into Hell. Cute.

There were posters splattered all over town announcing the gig that night: THE TROJANS LIVE TONIGHT IN HADES. The Trojans is the name of the band. Everyone thinks they named themselves after the condoms, but it is really the name of the football team in Wynokie, the next town over, where Oliver lives. Evan went to school there until he was a junior. Then his parents got divorced and he moved to Lenape with his father.

Hades was full of sweaty bodies wearing very little clothing, ready to party. Already the groupies had conquered the area closest to the stage. The groupies used to bother me until Jessie showed me how to handle them. Now I wear anti-groupie clothing: tiny skirt and plunging top; underneath, a garter belt with thigh-high stockings and thong; and, to top it off, bright red boots. Red boots can kick any groupies' butts if they start to swarm, and they always start to swarm.

Jessie and I pushed our way through the groupies so we were closest to the stage. We did this with authority and no groupie interfered. It was quite clear we were The Girlfriends. Evan always likes it when I am up front so he can see me from the stage, even though many times I'd rather just sit at a table and watch. Oliver waited until we were in place. He leaned into the mike. He said to the crowd: "Thanks for coming," and his voice reverberated through the club. Slowly he started rapping with no music; Evan kept the beat. The rap started building, building, growing more intense; Colin, the bass player, kicked in with a deep boom; José on the keyboards struck a chord. Then Oliver stopped. He played a riff. He started singing and wailing on the guitar and the other guys jumped in and the whole thing transformed into rock and roll. The crowd hooted and hollered.

Jessie and I moved to the beat. We worked our backs. We are both great dancers and all eyes were on us. We wiggled and swayed and held each other, and then we pulled apart. We raised our hands over our heads and clapped to the beat, moving our hips like serpents. *Stomp. Stomp.* I was Isis. *Clap. Clap.* She was Aphrodite. We were goddesses, swirling and dipping, hair tumbling through the air. The crowd followed us. *Clap. Clap. Stomp. Stomp.* The whole club was clapping and stomping to the music, clapping to the beat of Evan's drums. We stamped. We strutted. When the song was over, we kissed each other long and deep to tease the crowd, and everyone screamed and clapped. But this time, instead of enjoying the excitement, I remember stepping outside of myself, watching, and thinking that what used to be fun was turning into a chore.

Tonight Jessie is wearing an East Indian skirt down to her hips and an alter-top flossy kind of blouse. Oliver is dressed kind of like Evan, all in loose black cotton, except on him the clothes look radical. This is their "going to the city" garb.

Again, I am retelling the events of the day, and Jessie is shrieking, "No way! No WAY! NO WAY!" Oliver sits there, going, "Whoa. Cool. Whoa. No way. Whoa. Too much." I can see Evan's face in the rearview mirror; he is wearing a constant grin. He catches my eye and winks. Every so often, Sean turns around and looks back at us and says something, but he mostly lets me tell the story. I can tell he is not thrilled with being in the passenger's seat next to a younger man who is driving.

I get to the part about Peppy and Roger, and the atmosphere inside the car turns from sunshine to partly cloudy. The more detailed I get, the blacker the approaching storm becomes. Something inside tells me to stop, but my mouth keeps going. I say: "It turns out that Peppy got pregnant just to get out of the house. That she got involved with Sean because Roger was going out with some girl named Rosie."

There is a green Honda in front of us that is going too slowly, but we are wedged in between a tractor trailer on the right and a housewife in a minivan on the left who has almost, but not quite, worked up enough courage to pass. Evan keeps looking left, then right, then in the rearview mirror. He is getting frustrated. "Yeah. But still. Sean went back to Ronnie. Isn't that true?" Evan doesn't look at Sean when he says this, but it is clear the question is directed at him.

It feels weird to have Evan put Sean on the spot like this, in front of the pack; I wonder if he is feeling competitive. My first reaction is to stop the conversation. But then, I think it is about time we get the whole thing out in the open. Sean squirms; he is most definitely uncomfortable. He says, "It was one night. We were drunk. It was a mistake."

"Yeah, but that one mistake ended up being Carla. It was kind of a big mistake."

Evan keeps the pressure cranked up on Sean, and I am surprised; he's not usually like this. He steps on the gas, but the housewife in the minivan chooses that moment to speed up, too, and blocks us in. "Damn."

Sean looks out the window. "It was a *really* big mistake." He speaks to his reflection in the window.

Now I get a little upset. "I don't think Carla would appreciate being called 'a really big mistake.' If she's a really big mistake, what does that make me? At least Carla was conceived in passion. I was just a plot."

"Harley, I was stupid, all right? We were young. We

were drunk. Ronnie was familiar. She knew all the right moves." Sean starts getting agitated. "But I'm sitting here now, aren't I? I'm riding in the car with you. I am giving you my time. Let's not get into this."

Evan says, "Yeah, but you weren't there for sixteen years. That's a big chunk of time that you did not give to her. If you really cared about Harley, you would have broken down the door or something. I would have."

"You've never been in that position, Evan." Sean has been through too much today; his voice turns sharp. "After you're in that position, then we'll talk."

Yeah, well, Dad, Evan *is* in that position; it's just that he doesn't know it yet. For a wild moment, I think about blurting out in front of the entire automobile that I am pregnant, but I restrain myself. I can see the evening ahead turning into a disaster if we stay on this track. "Let's talk about something else," I say. "Let's talk about where we should park the car."

"No, no, I want to talk about this." Evan is oddly insistent. Maybe he is picking up on my dilemma; sometimes he can read my mind that way. "I want to know why you never went to see Harley. I have to live with it, too, you know."

That is the first time Evan has let on that my troubles affect him. I am torn between my feelings for him and the instinct to shield my father. Oliver, however, has no problem choosing sides and jumps right in. "Hey, man, Sean's right. Let's drop it. What's done is done. No point in talking about it."

Now Evan zeroes in on Oliver. "What, Oliver, let's just have another beer? What good does it do? My father has been married four times, and I'm sick of it."

Jessie's voice is pleading. "This is supposed to be a fun time. Let's keep this a fun time."

"Evan. Evan. What do you want me to say?" Sean looks like he wants to take off his seat belt and bolt. "I'm an asshole? Okay. I'm an asshole. Happy?"

Evan swerves into the left lane and floors it. He zooms in front of the housewife in the minivan with only inches to spare. We are all thrown sideways. "You think that's it? That's not it. I just want to know why." I think he is talking to his own father, not to Sean. The housewife in the minivan lays on her horn.

"Hey, man, take it easy." Oliver puts his hand on Evan's shoulder from behind.

"Hell, if I knew *why* . . ." Sean doesn't finish the sentence. "Why do you think I went back there today? I don't know why myself. What, do you think you get to be thirty, forty years old and all of a sudden you get all the answers? You don't get any answers. You just get more questions."

The car is silent. Then I say: "Hence the name of the Nicholas Raftner play." I pause. *"Answers."*

After a long beat, Sean laughs. "Good one, Harley." He chuckles. "Good one."

We pull into an open-air parking lot close to the Walter Kerr Theatre, where *Answers* is opening in four days. The rest of the conversation on the way to the city skidded along the surface, avoiding the depths, but there is still an underlying tension between us. Sean is nervous; I am nervous; our nerves are affecting the rest of the group.

Oliver opens the back door and lumbers out of the car. I follow behind. The New York City air hits me hard in the face. "Ah!" I take a deep breath. I listen to the traffic and the honking and the people shouting and feel the pulse of the city change the rhythm of my heart. The street noises are like listening to a favorite song. "It's so good to be back here." I don't use the word "home" because I am still not sure where, exactly, that is.

Jessie appears at my side. She gazes up at the skyscrapers, stately and imposing compared to the houses in Lenape. She voices my thoughts. "You are so lucky, Harley. To live here. You are so lucky to have gotten out of Lenape." I think: well, I'm not out yet, but I don't say this.

"We're only going to be an hour or so," Evan tells the parking-lot guy. "So I'd appreciate it if you left the car close to the front."

The parking-lot guy takes Evan's keys. "Yeah.

Yeah. Right, buddy. You and the rest of Manhattan. I'll see what I can do."

Sean takes out his wallet and hands the guy a ten-dollar bill. "Keep it close to the front. We don't want to be late to our next appointment. Okay?" Whenever Sean puts his Voice of Authority tone on, I am always impressed at the response. Already Sean seems like he is shedding the persona imposed upon him by suburbia; he is back in his element and takes control.

The parking lot guy examines the ten-dollar bill in his hand. He looks up at Sean. "Will do, boss."

The five of us scurry up Eighth Avenue, dodging the homeless and the elite, the out-of-towners and the born-and-bred. Sean leads the way, taking huge strides, and we follow as if he were the Pied Piper. I am having a very hard time keeping up in my heels, so I grab on to Evan's arm. We turn up West Forty-eighth Street and see the *Answers* marquee in the middle of the block. We hurry until we reach the theater. Right next to the main entrance, there is a small door with a single lightbulb overhead that apparently is the backstage door. Outside the door, two girls are whispering and giggling as if they are working up their nerve to walk inside.

Sean steps past the girls, and we follow him. He checks them out and keeps moving, waltzing right through the stage door. I see the look on the girls' faces turn to surprise, then envy, and I feel like a princess entering a castle. Sean descends the steps that lead to an East Indian man behind a small window reading the paper and drinking coffee from a Styrofoam cup. "Hey, Sam. The kids are with me." Sam looks up from his paper, nods, and then goes back to reading.

We trail Sean through the corridor, passing people that I am not sure are actors or part of the crew since everyone is in street clothes. There is a rack of costumes off to the right and a woman with a mouth full of pins kneeling next to it. She looks up and her eyes brighten; she mumbles through the pins and waves at Sean. Two guys dressed in work clothes pass by holding strange objects in their hands; one carries a stuffed porcupine and a lamp shade, the other a blender and a folding chair. One guy says, "Hey, Sean," and Sean says, "Hey, Larry." Everyone is bustling like they are doing something Very Important. It is totally exciting to be backstage in a Broadway theater. Even Oliver, who is normally unimpressed by anything, whispers to me, "This is too cool."

We pass a few people lounging by a water cooler. A really cute brunette calls out to Sean in a flirty voice, "Hey, Sean!"

Sean stops. He blinks and registers who she is. "Hi, Gloria. Come over here. I want you to meet my daughter."

"Daughter? You have a daughter?" Gloria has short brown hair all in ringlets and looks a little like Betty Boop with bright red lipstick. She's wearing a short skirt and four-inch heels and is showing a lot of cleavage. She looks me up and down. "It's got to be this one." She says this like she is on a Guess-My-Daughter quiz show. "She looks just like you. Hello there. I'm Gloria Mason." She offers her hand, all dainty and delicate. I shake it, and it is like shaking air.

"Gloria is understudying the three main leads," Sean says, and I realize that I am meeting the girl of condom fame. I am surprised that this is the type of woman Sean goes for; she looks like she crawled out of the pages of

Penthouse. He introduces our pack. "This is Evan, and Oliver, and . . . don't tell me . . . Jessica."

Gloria nods but doesn't offer her hand to the rest of the group. You can tell she hasn't listened to anyone's names, and Sean has neglected to even mention mine. She fixates on Sean. "You know what Melanie said to me? 'Break a leg!' " Gloria leans in to Sean and speaks in a loud whisper. "That bitch. I wanted to say break yours, too, I *wish*— break both! but I didn't."

Sean chuckles. "Melanie plays the lead," he says to us. "And Gloria is being catty."

"Catty? She's two sizes bigger than me. Who ever heard of a leading lady that looks like a blimp? I am sure Frank Povero will point that out. He never says anything good about her since she dumped him."

"Frank Povero is a critic for the *Times*," Sean explains. "Regrettably addicted to adverbs." I watch him ogle Gloria's chest. "Is Melanie here yet?"

"Yeah, she's in the dressing room, probably eating a plate of lasagna. She's always stinking up the dressing room with garlic."

"Tonight's cue-to-cue. . . . Tech rehearsal," Sean clarifies. "That means the actors are here to set their lighting cues, do the blocking, et cetera. It's boring. They hate it."

"Well, Josephine has yet to grace us with her presence. You know I'll get stuck doing all her blocking. She's another one."

"Josephine is far from fat. I think she's thinner than you, Gloria."

"I didn't mean she was fat. I meant she was a bitch."

Sean grins. "You can see what kind of mood Gloria is in."

"Oh, I'm sorry." Gloria actually flutters her eyelashes at Sean. "I'm giving the kids a bad impression."

Oliver and Evan are busy staring at Gloria's chest. "Huh?" Oliver says.

Sean disentangles Gloria's arm from his waist. "I have to get going, Gloria. We're already running late. Rosemary is going to have my head."

"What are you doing later on? You want to eat something?" Gloria has dropped her voice to seductive mode. "You and the kids, of course."

Sean hesitates. "Another time. Harley has an art exhibit tonight."

"Harley? Who's Harley? You know I don't know much about art."

I step up to Gloria and look her in the eye. "I'm Harley. His daughter. Remember?"

Gloria giggles, undaunted. "Oh! Silly me! I thought it was an artist or something."

Now Evan speaks up. "Harley *is* an artist. She's a great artist. She has a show opening tonight at Beatrice Snow's gallery down in Chelsea."

"Forgive me, Harley." Gloria segues perfectly, and I am impressed. She takes my hand and says very sincerely, "Break a leg," and I think it won't be long before she is playing the lead in *Answers and* christening the condoms.

We are sitting in the fifth row of the orchestra section because Sean wants us out of the way. Everybody inside the theater seems on edge. The set looks fantastic, but I am not sure how they are going to turn a living room into a boat, and, from the sound of it, neither are they. The conversations seem to be going like this:

"Damn it, Felix, I said move it to the right, not to the left!"

"Screw you."

The theater is old-fashioned. Art Deco. We're transported back to the 1920s just by being inside. It's all pink and mauve with chandeliers dangling and sconces lighting up the walls. It seems even smaller than the high school auditorium in Lenape. The seats we sit in are cushioned but not very comfortable; there isn't much room for people's legs and Oliver's knees are jammed up against the seat in front of him. On stage, the set is mostly blue, a vivid deep-sea blue—the color of my eyes, the color of Sean's eyes. There is a living room to the left with a sofa and a rocking chair. To the right is a kitchen complete with a refrigerator; water really comes out of the faucet in the sink. A couple of actors have wandered onto the stage with scripts in their hands. They walk through their paces while the crew maneuvers around them, and I think it is strange that such a thing as The Theater exists. Sean is up onstage, and he seems like another person entirely; he has transformed into a gear of a magnificent machine.

I remember once when Sean had a night off and it was dinner at home with just the two of us. He was cooking some mishmash of hot, spicy food in the wok. It was sort of Mexican-Chinese, his own invention, with vegetables, chicken, jalapeño peppers, and soy sauce. He was singing along to a song from *La Bohème*, his favorite opera. "Do you know why I love my job, Harley?"

I adored it when he was like this, an exotic father imported from a heaven abroad. There was nothing better than to be the object of Sean's attention when his spotlight was focused on you. "Why?"

"I work with four dimensions. There are the usual three, plus another: time. Think about it."

I thought about it. "I don't get it." The tenor was singing, soaring, intense, in the background. I couldn't understand the words but his heart seemed to be breaking.

"When the audience arrives, we are in the little box of the theater; the show starts at eight o'clock. I create the space. I create the illusion of the space that they have stepped into. From eight o'clock to eleven, whenever, for three hours, for that time, in that space, reality is what is there on stage. It can't exist in a movie because you are removed; it's celluloid; the actors aren't there; the space is not there; it is a beautiful illusion, that's all. It can't exist in television; it is so far away that it is like junk food. Television feels real because strangers are broadcast into your living room, because you see them in your home. But they are inside an electronic box; they are removed.

"But the theater . . . four dimensions exist in the theater because the space is really there; the actors are really there; they are really feeling that emotion at that moment, in that time; it is really happening right there in that time, in that space. And if it's good, the audience feels the same emotion that the actor feels. It's different every night because the audience is different every night. The audience affects the actors and the actors affect the audience. The theater is real. Opera is real. Better than real. Get it?"

I nodded, moved. "Got it."

I think of that conversation now as I watch a woman up on the stage dressed all in black whose name is Rosemary; she has purple highlights in her hair and speaks with dominion. Sean introduced us to her earlier as the stage manager. Sean and Rosemary stand in a spotlight in center stage and bicker. I am not sure whether we are watching a comedy or a drama.

"There's not enough time to move the sofa off," Rosemary says. "And even if there was, there's no place to put it backstage, you've got so much crap back there."

"What are you talking about? Where's Aldo?" Sean shouts. "Aldo!"

A voice backstage yells, "Aldo's not here!"

Another voice emanates from the loudspeakers like the voice of God. "Who the hell touched my board?" The lights on stage turn from red, to blue, to green. "Did someone mess with my board? I need someone down there to flag the green spot."

Someone yells back: "Take it easy, Hank! No one touched your goddamn board!" There are disembodied voices coming from every direction.

"Sean, will ya flag the green spot?"

Sean is still talking to Rosemary. Without missing a beat, he walks into the beam of the green spotlight and waves his hand. "Maybe we can create the boat with the sofa still onstage, just moved off to the side or something. Since we have to end up right back in the living room. That could work."

At that moment, music starts blaring. "Turn down the music!" Sean yells into the theater. "We're trying to have a conversation here."

Oliver leans over and says to Evan, "Sounds like the band at a sound check, eh, bro?"

A short guy with a bald head comes scurrying up to

Sean. "Whaddya want?"

"What do you mean, what do I want, Aldo? I want a ham and Swiss on rye." Sean stays calm. "I want to know why the sofa doesn't fit backstage."

At that moment, a heavyset woman enters the orchestra section holding a bunch of papers. She has a beautiful face, but her body is definitely plump. "Where's Nicholas? I want to change this line." She says this to nobody in particular. She looks around the theater and sees the four of us sitting there. "Who are you?"

We all look at each other. Oliver shrugs. Evan looks away. Jessie giggles. I decide to answer. I stand up. "Hello, my name is Harley Columba. I'm Sean Shanahan's daughter."

The woman doesn't offer her hand. Instead, she calls up to Sean, "Sean, since when do we have guests at cue-to-cue? I thought there were no guests at cue-to-cue."

Sean puts his hand up to his eyes to shield them from the glare of the spotlight. "Melanie, is that you? That's my daughter. They're only staying for a few minutes and then we're heading out."

"If I knew we could have guests at cue-to-cue, I would have brought my boyfriend. Where's Nicholas?"

"Nicholas is running late," says Rosemary, glancing at her watch.

"Where's Garth?" Melanie rolls the papers into a cylinder and starts whacking the backs of the seats. Garth Gallo is the director; Sean thinks he's brilliant.

"Garth is around somewhere," Rosemary says. "I think he's in the booth."

"Garth went to the john," says the voice of God. "I think he fell in."

"Go look for him, Melanie. It's going to be a while before we need you. If you find him, tell him we need him. Pronto." Rosemary turns back to Sean and Aldo. "So what are you going to do about the sofa?"

"Oh, Christ, how I hate cue-to-cue." Melanie is dramatic; she swishes through the curtains on the left.

"Hank, can we see the lights for the boat scene?" Sean asks. He puts on a headset and speaks into a microphone. "Hank. Hank. Are you there? I want to check something." He takes off the headset. "It's not working." He shouts. "Hank!"

The voice of God answers back. "Yeah. What?" There is high, screechy feedback with curses underneath. "Something is wrong with the headsets. The boat scene? Now? I have the lights ready for the first scene. It's out of order."

"I've got to run, so can we please do it out of order? I need to see them."

"You've got to run? You've got to *run*? It's cue-to-cue,

for crissake, and you've got to run? You're the goddamn set designer, Sean."

"I spoke to Garth. Aldo is here. Aldo can handle it." Sean turns to Aldo. "Right, Aldo?"

Aldo shrugs. "You're the boss."

Sean takes a deep breath but there is frustration in his voice. "You're right. I am." He shields his eyes again from the spotlight. "Harley, are you out there?"

I am startled. "Yes." I stand up.

"Come on up here." I am surprised, but I obey. I head up the steps at the back and walk onto the stage. The floor is wood, polished and shiny. It is a strange sensation standing up here in front of all the seats, even if they are empty; surreal, as if I were walking into another reality. My black spikes *click, click, click* on the wooden floor. I am aware of my footsteps, my body; my senses are suddenly heightened.

"I heard that, you know, Peggy," says the voice of God. For a moment, I think he is talking to me.

"Heard what?" asks a female voice from the stage.

"What you whispered. You're right under the mike."

I move to where Sean is, in the center. I can see why he is blinded; the spotlight dissolves all but the front row of the theater into black. Everything onstage, however, is bright and clear. Workers are bustling, actors are mumbling; there is a cute guy sitting on a stool behind the curtain drinking coffee. I am in a living room, but there are no walls, and there are other beings moving through the space. I trip over an electrical cord as I approach Sean talking with Rosemary. An alternate world is going on up here, and I am not sure whether I have walked into a scene from someone else's play.

Rosemary frowns. "Sean, this isn't a family outing."

"Rosemary, please." Sean's voice has an edge. He puts his hands on my shoulders. "Harley, listen. There is no way I am going to be able to make it down to Chelsea right now. Maybe I can get away later. Do you understand? You're going to have to go without me. Okay?"

I am so disappointed; I feel the tears sting my eyes. I try to hold them back. I nod. "Yes." My voice is a peep.

"Don't look at me that way. Don't make me feel guilty."

"What do you expect me to look like? I wanted you to come, okay?" I am surprised myself at how upset I feel. I had built my expectations up so high that it is like a skyscraper crumbling down.

A stagehand walks past with a long wooden plank and accidentally hits me on the shoulder. "Sorry," he says, and keeps moving.

At that moment, the world turns dark. Shafts of light flicker across the stage like the moon hitting the waves of the sea. The sound of water sloshes. The living room transforms into a boat. Even though we stand in the same place, suddenly we are inside the hull of a ship and I am drowning. . . .

"How's that, Sean?" the voice of God rumbles. "Is that okay?"

"Give me a minute, Hank!" Sean says. He starts pacing. Spokes flash across his face, bright, then dark; bright, then dark. The boat rocks one way, then another. "You can see that it's just not possible. You can see that I am needed here."

"I need you, too." The words tumble out of my mouth before I can stop them. I am below the deck; I have lost all sense of direction; I don't know which way the ship is moving.

"Give you a *minute*?" The voice of God throws a few thunderbolts down from the light booth. "You ask me to skip to the third act and now you want a minute? Sean, I hate to tell you, but you are not the star of this show."

"Damn it, Sean, we're on a tight schedule here!" Rosemary jumps into our scene. "Where is Garth?"

Thunder cracks. Lightning flashes. Sean has reached his limit and explodes. "*This* is what I've been trying to get through your head, Harley. I don't have time to be a father! I don't have time to be your pal!" His lightning strikes my heart and I am dizzy. Even Sean seems shocked at the bolts that have shot out of his mouth. He takes a deep breath and struggles for control. "I'm sorry, Harley, but this is my job and there are a lot of people depending on me to do it well. There is a lot of money riding on this show. It is opening in four days. An audience is arriving. They have bought their tickets. You are not a child. You have your friends with you. Go to the exhibit and if I can, I will try to make it later on."

"If you don't have dinner with the understudy!" I don't know what's come over me. I am being totally unreasonable but I can't stop. All the tensions of the day have piled up into one blazing scene. The dark stage bursts into brightness and a red light illumines Sean's face. He is furious.

"That's it! Really, Harley. I've had it! I haven't had a day like today in my entire life. The two of us living together just isn't working. Now go downtown to your exhibit so I can concentrate. That is the end of this conversation." A huge swell crashes on top of us and the ship is sinking. . . .

I am full-out crying now. The tempest is inside me; the saltwater pours out my eyes and into my mouth. "I had a rough day, too, you know! All you think about is yourself! I am sure you are not the only set designer in the world who has a daughter!" I choke on my tears. I storm to the back of the stage and fly down the steps. I stumble and reach for a railing that doesn't exist. For a moment, I think I am going to soar headfirst off into space. Man overboard. Man overboard. I catch my balance, pause, and wobble out into the audience. My palms reverberate pins and needles from the near fall. The music swells, the lights dissolve from red to green. Sean and Rosemary remain motionless on stage as the lights dim, then fade to black.

Somewhere in the darkness of the theater one person starts clapping.

I am still tearful as we walk to the parking lot. Jessie's got her arm around me and tries to comfort me. "Yes, Harley. Yes, it was hurtful of Sean to do that to you in front of the whole theater. But the stage is like his home. It's normal for him. I'm sure he didn't think about how it would affect you."

"He only thinks about himself."

"Yeah, Sean's got an ego, but you could see everyone was putting pressure on him. You're taking this way too personally. I think your father's great. Crazy, but great. He was cool enough to let us come in the first place. He does have to do the show. So do you. Concentrate on yourself. You've worked so hard for this. Don't let it get ruined."

Evan and Oliver walk in front of us. They are silent. Evan has his hands in his pockets. We pass a homeless guy passed out against a building, an empty bottle of bourbon by his side. Oliver points to the guy and says, "Look at the bright side. Things could be worse. You could be him."

Jessie nips at him. "Oliver, now is not the time for your twisted sense of humor."

"Lighten up, Jess. It's just a family squabble. You should hear my parents blast into me. You'd think I was some prehistoric slug that crawled up from the bowels of the earth. I just block them out. I pop another tune on the jukebox, baby, and put on the ol' head-set. It'll blow over. Tomorrow everything will be fine."

Now Evan is alongside me. "You know, Harley, you should listen to Jessie. I don't know what's happening to you. You were so excited about your exhibit. Now look at you. What changed? Because Sean can't make it? It's not the end of the world. I'm here. Jessie and Oliver are here. Whenever you're with Sean, you're different."

I look up at him through my tears. He is out of focus. "What do you mean?"

Evan shrugs. "I don't know. It's like you idolize him or something. It's weird. He's just a guy with a cool job, not Jesus Christ."

We arrive at the parking lot. Evan's Camaro is actually parked right in front. I think it wouldn't be parked there if it hadn't been for Sean. "Sean got your car up front."

Evan snorts. "Big deal. All it took was ten bucks. It's not like he parted the Red Sea or something."

"Evan's got a point, Harley," Jessie says. "Maybe you don't know it, but you act like somebody else when you're around Sean. I never saw you like that before." She tries to soften her words by touching my arm, but I pull away.

"Why is everybody picking on me?" I start crying again. "Why are you all turning against me? Only good things have been happening since I've known Sean. You're turning into strangers!"

"Chill out, Harley," Oliver chimes in. "Nobody's pick-ing on you. We're just trying to get you to see reality."

"Yeah, well, maybe my reality is changing." My words are like a slap that hangs in the air.

Evan pays the parking-lot attendant. The attendant starts toward the car, but Evan stops him. "Just give me the keys and I'll drive it off the lot. We're kind of in a hurry."

The attendant gives Evan a look but hands over the keys. "Careful you don't hit another car backing out, kid."

Evan holds two dollars in his hand that he was going to give the attendant as a tip. Instead, he very deliberately opens his wallet and puts the money back inside. The attendant watches this but says nothing. "Come on," Evan says. "Let's get out of here."

We all pile in the car, Jessie and me in the backseat and the boys in the front. Evan puts the key in the ignition and the Camaro roars to life. "Okay. Where are we going?"

I pull the bright red postcard out of my handbag. **life never stops. .** Ha. It seems to me like life has ground to a halt now that Sean is not coming to my exhibition. "West Twenty-fourth Street," I sniff.

Evan pulls out of the lot without a scratch, turns onto Seventh Avenue, and heads downtown. There is so much traffic we are barely crawling. Evan pulls into the right lane and gets blocked immediately by a taxi letting off some passengers. "Stay in the middle, bro," says Oliver. "It's better that way."

"You want to drive, Oliver?" Evan glances over his shoulder, trying to change lanes, but no one lets him in.

"Fix your makeup, Harley," Jessie encourages. "We'll be there in plenty of time." She takes a brush from her handbag and runs it through my hair. Stroke. Stroke. Her action is familiar. . . . I close my eyes. Stroke. Stroke. Like a paintbrush in my hair. . . . I start to drift away. . . . I try to force us all into a painting but get trapped inside a memory instead. . . . I am backstage in a dressing room alone, sitting at the table, staring in a mirror. Evan's band is onstage; the music pounds through the walls. My head throbs.

"What's wrong, Harley?"

I look up. Jessie has come into the room. She is wearing a T-shirt that says I'M WITH THE BAND. She sweeps the beer bottles and chips and candy on the table into a tidy pile and sits next to me.

"Did you see the blond?" I ask her. "She's all over Evan. And he's going for it."

Jessie takes a brush out of her purse and starts smoothing my hair as if I am a lonely child she can stroke into happiness. "Yeah, I saw her. Solution: fix your makeup, Harley. Put on some lipstick and let's go out and dance. Have a better time than he is. Trust me."

"I'm getting tired of it."

"You think it's bad now? Wait until the album comes out."

"She's a bimbo."

"That's why you need your own life. You're an artist, Harley. You need to do what you do. Evan needs to do what he does. Face it. He's a drummer in a rock band. It's a crazy life and it's just going to get crazier. I like it. You don't. I'm happy going with the pack, being Ollie's girl. You've got things to think about." The music stops. The crowd applauds. "Come on, girlfriend. Let's dance."

Now I can feel Jessie brushing my hair, but I don't know where I am. I am caught inside the memory and struggle to escape. Then I realize that we are in the car, not backstage. We are driving to my exhibit. There will be no dancing tonight for this girlfriend. I accept the tissue that Jessie hands me and blow my nose. I force myself to focus. All my realities are crashing into each other and I am in a daze. I remove my compact from my purse. "Let me hold that." Jessie's voice is far away. She takes the mirror and positions it in front of my face. I force myself to look into my eyes. They are murky, not eager; they are someone else's eyes. Something is definitely wrong, but I don't know what it is. I take out my makeup bag and start to apply some foundation. I dab an extra swab onto my red nose. I sniff. I whimper.

"Harley, knock it off, will you?" Evan finally gets an opening and wedges the Camaro in between a taxi and an approaching bus. "I'm trying to concentrate."

Evan's voice is like a spank that forces me totally into the present. I don't understand why he is being mean now, too. "I'm trying, Evan!" My voice is whiny. I have regressed to infancy.

"The guy wasn't even around while you were growing up, and now you've turned him into a saint." Really, why is Evan so hostile about Sean? Then he says: "How do you think it makes me feel, seeing you all upset because your father isn't coming tonight, while I'm right here? Oliver and I left rehearsal early, you know."

"I'm sorry, Evan." I start sniffling again. "I appreciate that you are here, I really do."

"Come on, Evan, don't you start in on her, too." Jessie lifts the hair off my shoulders and lets it tumble down my back.

"I'm sorry, but I think Sean is a real jerk. Knocking up Peppy, knocking up Ronnie, and running off. Didn't they have condoms back then?" Evan taps his fingers on the steering wheel, nervous, like it is his drum.

"Maybe they got wrapped up in the passion of the

moment. It does happen, Evan," I say through my whimpers. I can't believe he is criticizing Sean for doing the same thing we did.

"We always use condoms."

Apparently, he has deleted last month's lovemaking session completely from his memory bank. Now I start getting mad. "That's not true! No we don't!"

"Only once we didn't." So he does remember; he just chooses to omit it.

"Yeah, well, once was enough!" The words burst out of my mouth and end in a sob.

There is silence in the car. "What do you mean?" Evan says this quietly.

I am crying again. I have turned into a natural disaster. "I think I'm pregnant. I didn't get my period." On either side of me, I feel alarm radiate off Jessie and Oliver, and I am sorry I said this in front of them.

Jessie is shocked. "Oh my God. How late is it?"

"Five days."

"Five days isn't too bad," Oliver comments. "Jess, you didn't get it for like a week once, remember? We were kind of frantic."

"Did you use a condom?" I hope the answer is no.

"Yeah . . ." Oliver fidgets. "But still. It makes you nervous."

"Yeah, well, we didn't." I say this accusingly to Evan.

"I pulled out." Evan gets defensive. I can't believe he is justifying the same thing he was criticizing Sean for just hours before.

"You pulled out because Sean came home! And it's not like you had everything under control, Evan. Sperm can swim, you know. I read it on the Internet."

"I thought you were taking the pill, Harley," says Jessie.

"I stopped. It was giving me zits." I am getting a little crazy. "What do you say about it now, Evan? You want to be a father?"

Evan doesn't respond. He just taps on the steering wheel.

"Well, do you? Do you want to get married and have a little Harley or a little Evan?"

Evan does not respond.

"Evan, why aren't you answering me?"

"No."

I wait for him to elaborate. He does not. "No?" I push him. "Just like that? No?"

"Absolutely positively not. No way. No. It's not happening."

"Without even talking about it?"

"I don't have to talk about it. I already know." He floors the Camaro, trying to make it through the last breath of a yellow light. It turns red. He slams on the brakes and ends up blocking the crosswalk. "Look at you. Look at me. Look at the four of us. Do you think I'm going to bring a kid into the world at my age? Are you crazy? Look at our parents, for crissake. None of them are close to normal. I don't know if I ever want to have kids."

"Well, maybe you should think about that the next time we don't use a condom! Maybe you should try to resist!"

"I didn't see you stopping anything! Don't lay all this on me."

"You're the one who won't deal with it. I'm trying to deal with it. What do you think, I'm going to have an abortion?"

"There is no other option." His words echo into silence. A river of pedestrians floods our car on all sides, most of them giving us dirty looks for infringing on their ability to navigate the crosswalk.

"No other option?" I repeat his words.

"That's right. No other option for me. Have a baby, if you want. Have it by yourself. I don't want one. I'm telling you right now. I am a musician. We are about to record an album. You don't get a shot like that every day. I'll be damned if I'm going to let a baby mess that up. No way." A guy with dreadlocks pounds on the hood of the Camaro because he can't get past. "Screw you!" Evan hollers through the window. He turns to Oliver. "You got any weed, bro?"

Oliver nods. "Yeah."

Jessie says, "I thought we weren't going to smoke any pot tonight. I thought we were going to be proper."

Evan shrugs. "I changed my mind."

I can't believe Evan is behaving like this. It's like he's another person entirely, a stranger behind the wheel and I am in the wrong car. Without thinking, I open the car door and jump out into the middle of Seventh Avenue. At that moment, the light turns green and Evan is forced to move forward. I dodge the traffic and the honking horns and the squealing brakes until I make it to the curb. Then I stumble to the sidewalk and sob.

I take a breath and try to pull myself together. I wipe my nose. Focus, Harley, focus. Time. What is the time? I stop a sophisticated couple walking arm in arm. They look well organized; one of them will certainly be wearing a watch. "Excuse me, do you know what time it is?" My voice sounds frenetic.

Sure enough, the man pushes up his sleeve and exposes his Rolex. "Seven thirty-seven exactly."

"Thanks." I think fast. I look up Seventh Avenue. For as far as I can see, none of the taxis has its AVAILABLE sign lit up, and there are already two people out in the street with their hands in the air, trying to hail a cab. Plus, the traffic is moving so slowly, the odds are I won't make it down to Chelsea on time. It's too far to walk in spike heels. There is only one option. The subway. I am close to the subway. If I take the No. 1 down to Twenty-third Street, I can catch a taxi from there. If I get lucky, I will make it to the gallery by eight. It is the only solution.

Clackety-clack. The No. 1 subway train clatters down the track. I am wedged in between an old Jewish guy wearing a yarmulke on my left and an old Muslim guy wearing a big Allah pendant around his neck on my right. I am the demilitarized zone. I feel completely overdressed for a ride in a subway car. I close my eyes and rock with the rhythm of the train. Again, I try to conjure up a painting, but the magic isn't working; this time I am propelled into the future. . . .

"Hey, Harley." I am in bed alone and Evan's voice wakes me up. "I'm home." His words are slurred and I think he is drunk. Tiny Christopher, named after Sean's stepfather, lies in his cradle at the foot of the bed and starts crying.

"What time is it?"

"I dunno. Four? Five?" Evan takes off his leather boots and drops them with a thud on the floor.

"Evan, you woke up the baby."

"So feed him or something."

I click on the light by the nightstand. Shadows fall on our little apartment, exposing the crumbling plaster from the radiator leak upstairs. Evan yanks his black T-shirt over his head. It smells like beer.

"What's that on your neck?" I ask. The hardwood

floor is cold against my bare feet. I take Christopher out of his cradle and bounce him, trying to quiet his wails.

"Jeez, he's got a pair of lungs. Can't you do something?"

"I asked what was on your neck. It looks like lipstick."

"Harley, I'm exhausted. We played three encores tonight."

"I'm tired, too, Evan!" Christopher is shrieking now. I pat him on the back. "I'm supposed to finish a portrait by Tuesday, and it's only half done. I don't have time to do anything but take care of Christopher."

"Don't nag me, Harley. I don't want to come home and hear you bitch. You wanted that kid. You got him. Deal with it."

I don't like that image. I open my eyes. Sitting directly across from me in the subway car is a skinny white guy staring at me with a strange look on his face. He does not look away when I meet his eyes. Instead, he smiles a salacious smile. Gross. I look away. I examine the other people on the train; they are all vacant behind their eyes. I look back at the skinny guy. He is still staring at me. He mouths the words "I want you" very slowly and licks his lips. I stab him with my eyes, and then look away.

"... I tell you I died, I was dead, I literally died." I realize that the Muslim guy is speaking to the Jewish guy and I have accidentally sat in the middle of their conversation. The Jewish guy is listening and nodding his head. The Muslim guy says, "My heart stopped. They used those things on me to jump-start it, like a car. I was in darkness, almost like a tunnel. Up ahead, I saw a white light, just like you hear about. It was so bright it frightened me. I knew I had to go inside it to get to the other side. I didn't want to. It hurt to look at it, but it didn't cast its rays on me. I tried to back into the light, to jump through it backward, but instead of going through, I ended up right back where I started, in a dark tunnel."

"What happened to you?" asks the Jewish guy. "How did you die?"

I am riveted by their conversation. Both men are looking straight ahead, not at each other, so I look straight ahead, too, careful to avoid eye contact with the weirdo across the aisle, and listen.

"Gunshot," says the Muslim guy with no further explanation. "So I am right back where I started and I think, I want to see my daughter again. I was not a good father, and if I die in the dark, I will never be able to fix things with her. If I can get to the light, I know I get another chance, but if I die in the dark, then I'm dust."

The Jewish guy asks, "Another chance?"

"I just felt it," says the Muslim guy. "So I start again toward the light. I walk quickly using my arms, power walking but not running. This time, when I get to the light, I force myself to jump right through without stopping. And you know what was on the other side?"

I think: What? The Jewish guy says: "What?"

"A grassy meadow, rolling hills, with lots of animals. Dangerous animals mixed up with other animals, animals that would normally eat each other, but all together, really peaceful. There were panthers, coyotes, and . . . snakes. Bears. Deer. An alligator was in a pond with an otter and a beaver. The sun was shining and there were hawks and songbirds in the sky. There was a wooden bridge over a gully in the middle of the meadow. I knew I had to cross it. I passed this big elk and this little mouse. I started across the bridge, and then I saw that a bear was coming at me from the other direction, walking, standing up. We met in the middle and I became frightened again, so I pushed him off. He looked at me before he fell over the side, and his eyes were full of . . . sadness. Compassion. He wasn't angry that I had pushed him, and I was immediately sorry I did it. He fell over the side, and I looked down and saw that he had the head of a bear but the body of a man." The Muslim guy pauses.

"And then what happened?" I ask. It is rude to jump into their conversation, but I think this is one of the most incredible stories I have ever heard. The Muslim guy doesn't seem to mind. He is calm, matter-of-fact.

"Then I woke up and saw all these hospital people around me. Everybody dressed in white."

"Lotsa stories about that white light," says the Jewish guy. "Must be something to it."

I come up out of the subway on the corner of Twenty-third Street and Seventh Avenue. The Muslim guy's story has improved my spirits. The weather above-ground is fine—cool and crisp, as if a master hand had just wiped the air clean. I refresh my lungs and pause. I feel like something is missing. I have my purse but realize I have left my Gucci bag in the car. I wonder where Evan is, but I don't have time to think about it. I use all my strength to focus and grind the gears of my mind forward to the events at hand; my dignity returns. First step: taxi. I don't have to wait long before three yellow cabs approach. I step into the street and raise my hand and the first taxi beelines off course and halts so that the back door is almost touching my hand. I open it and climb in.

"529 West Twenty-fourth Street," I say. "Just down the block."

The taxi driver is a thin, white-haired guy, one of those drivers who have been on the job for centuries. The strange thing about him is that he is wearing a suit and tie. "Ya going to one of those art exhibitions?"

I am surprised. "Yes. How did you know?"

The driver laughs. "Honey, there ain't nothing else down there. Used to be there wasn't *nothing* down there. Now all you youngsters made yourselves a little art happening thing down there." He has a gravelly voice that still sounds warm. "I like that. I like it when the young people turn an area around. Me, I'm from Brooklyn. Park Slope. It's so hotsy-totsy where I live now, I had to buy new clothes just to stay in the neighborhood. It's nice. I like it. I needed some new clothes. How do you like my suit?"

"It's very stylish." It actually is quite nice, although I have never seen a cabbie wearing a suit and tie before. "I have a new dress, too."

"I used to dress like a slob, but my wife started cheating on me. So I changed my look. Gave her some romance— flowers, chocolate, the works. Now she's got dinner on the stove when I get home. What art you seeing tonight?"

Apparently, he is one of those conversational cabbies, and I am happy for the distraction. "Actually . . ." I hesitate, then go for it. "Actually, it's me. I am the artist. It's my exhibition. My first one."

The driver whistles. "Whoo-ee. That so? Honey, forgive me, but you don't seem old enough to hold a paintbrush. Or are you one of those con-tem-pry artists that doesn't believe in a brush?"

"Oh, I believe in a brush. I'm traditional that way. I paint with oil, actually."

"Well, I admire that. I respect that. I admire a kid like you, so young, painting something so good that you are in a hotsy-totsy Chelsea art gallery." He is sincere.

"Thank you." I am sincere, too.

The driver goes all the way down to Eleventh Avenue and makes a left. "What's your subject matter? What do you paint?"

"I do a lot of portraits. I do a lot of faces, but . . . I don't know, in a different kind of way. They are not portraits of real people all the time. Sometimes people I see in my head. I do portraits of real people, too, but I try to capture their essence, not their actual face. Well, it is their actual face the way I see it, but with their essence. It's sort of like a feeling, not an exact representation, though I can do exact portraits if I want. Like I have this one of George Washington, and across his forehead are the bodies of the mutineers that he had executed. Or there's one of John Lennon, and his glasses are shattered on his face to symbolize his murder, but he is glowing with a halo. There are sunbeams and a bunch of puffy number nines floating around the sky like clouds because nine is a mystical number, and it's like he has died and gone to heaven. Stuff like that. And there's an angel, for example." I realize I am rambling and think I must be very nervous. I gulp in some more air.

"Sounds good. Sounds very interesting. Here we are." The driver pulls up in front of a gray modern building. In fact, there are rows and rows of gray modern buildings, all the same, with little staircases that lead up to glass doors. There is one difference about this building, however: people are everywhere. I was here once before, during the day, to deliver my Life Never Stops entry and meet Beatrice Snow; then it was deserted. Now there are clumps of people on the staircase, on the sidewalk, spilling through the door. Most of them are dressed in black. "Looks like you got yourself quite a crowd."

I feel like telling him to turn around and take me home. "It's not possible." My words are a whisper. "Look at all those people."

"It's normal to be a little scared." The driver's voice is

soothing. "Don't ya have anybody to go in with you? Where're your friends? Where's your family?"

"I'm . . . alone." I swallow. "It's a long story."

"Well, heck, honey. Ya want me to go in with you? I can leave the cab here for a minute or two. Ya want me to? Those paintings you describe, well, I wouldn't mind having a look-see. I like art. Don't know too much about it except to say, yes, I like this, or no, I don't like that. I ain't sophisticated like most of those folks, but I do have these new clothes. And I do live in Park Slope." He chuckles. "My name's Joe, by the way. Joe Walesa. Of Polish descent."

"I'm Harley Columba. But my father's name is Shanahan. Sean Shanahan. He's a set designer on Broadway. He has to work tonight. His show is opening in four days." I hesitate. Now that we are here, all I feel is terror at the thought of walking in there alone. "Do you mind coming in? Just for a minute? I would like you to see my paintings, and I think they have some food."

Joe chuckles again. "I would like to see your paintings." He pats his stomach. "But I think my wife's been feeding me enough food." Joe parks at the curb and turns off the taxi. He gets out and opens the back door for me. He makes a little bow and a sweep of his hand, as if I were a star arriving at the Academy Awards. I put my heels to the pavement. Joe offers his arm and we step out into the night.

Beatrice Snow is waiting at the door. She looks exactly like her name: frosty hair, white skin, red lipstick, black suit.

"There you are! I was beginning to get worried. I thought perhaps tragedy had struck."

"No, no, everything's fine." I manage a smile.

"Is this your father? Is this Sean Shanahan?" Beatrice Snow turns to Joe, her red lipstick a frame around two rows of white teeth. I have never seen teeth that white; I think she bleaches them.

"No, ma'am, I'm Joseph Walesa. I'm a friend. Harley's father has a show opening in four days and, unfortunately, he is delayed at the theater. Technical rehearsal. He sends his regrets." I turn to look at Joe, amazed. All of a sudden, he sounds like he has graduated from Harvard. Joe leans over and whispers to me: "I used to be an actor."

Beatrice Snow looks disappointed. "Oh well. The show must go on, as they say. I was looking forward to meeting him." She turns to the crowd. "In any event, tonight is *your* show, Harley, and I am enthused that there are some very important people here in addition to the usual freeloaders. There is a critic from the *Times,* a critic from the *Art Newspaper,* a critic from the *New Yorker;* we are dripping with critics tonight. We even have a dear friend of mine in town from Venice, Malcolm Bryce Emerson, a British art critic who writes for the *International Tribune*. In fact, here he is. Come. I'll introduce you."

Beatrice Snow takes my hand and sweeps me into the crowd. There is music playing in the background, sort of bluesy rock, and I wonder who the artist is. "Who is that singing?" I ask.

"That's Spencer Davis. He's a very dear friend of mine." She tugs me toward a brown-haired man in a rumpled suit. I think Beatrice Snow has more very dear friends than anyone I've ever met, but when she introduces me to Malcolm Bryce Emerson, he does seem genuinely glad to meet me. "Mal, this is Harley, the artist."

"Lovely show, Harley." Malcolm's blue eyes crinkle behind his spectacles. "Impressive work."

I remember what Sean said about being gracious when receiving compliments. "Thank you." I hope my face is not red, but it feels hot, like I might be the victim of a blush despite my effort to remain cordial and composed. I realize that Joe has let go of my arm and has wandered off to look at the paintings and that I am standing here alone talking to an art critic from the *International Tribune,* and my world has again turned surreal.

"I especially like the one you've entered into competition, the pregnant angel. Where did you get the idea?"

"Um . . . uh . . ." I can see the headline now: THIS MONTH'S WINNER OF THE YOUNG ARTIST OF THE MONTH AWARD A BLITHERING IDIOT.

I pull myself together. "It just came to me. I was thinking about the theme, Life Never Stops, and life seemed like an embryo. An embryo comes from Eros—I've been studying the gods—that's why I put that little flame. So I started with the embryo inside the girl and the flame in the embryo's mouth instead of a tongue." The music changes; now it sounds like something Robin Hood would listen to when wandering in Sherwood Forest. I take a breath. "And then I put the tree around her because . . . well, it's sort of like the Tree of Life. And then . . . well, the next thing I knew, there was an angel in the sky with an embryo inside *her*, the same embryo with a little flame. And then she reached down and touched the girl with music, and the girl's song reached up, like they are sharing the same octave. But, honestly, I can't say it was something I really thought about. It just came out that way."

Malcolm turns to Beatrice Snow. He says: "Clever, this one," and I think my ramble might have been okay. But he is British; maybe he's just being polite.

Beatrice Snow's smile is blinding. "I do have an eye, darling," she says to Malcolm. She takes my hand again. "I do have an eye."

An older blond woman saunters over to our group. She has a face that looks like it was bought piece by piece; it is all perfect, but none of it really matches. "Beatrice, darling. Fabulous show. Just fabulous." She's got diamonds sparkling like tiny galaxies from four different fingers wrapped around a glass of champagne. "The best yet."

Beatrice Snow seems a little annoyed at the interruption. "Hello, Candace dear. Would you like to meet the artist?"

Candace pretends she is startled that I am standing right there. "Is this Harley Columba? Darling, you're so talented! I adore the one with the woman holding a mask in front of her face, all that yellow hair streaming out behind her. I'm going to buy it."

"Really?" I am so surprised, the words pop out of my mouth.

"Well, that's what we're here for, aren't we?"

Beatrice Snow says, "Harley, this is Candace Eastman. Candace is a major collector. She has excellent taste."

Malcolm mutters into my ear. "She's got too much money and no life. Associating with artists gives her a raison d'être." He says out loud: "If you'll excuse me, I see one of my colleagues over by the wine. Cheers."

Candace is still talking. "I always am on the lookout for new talent. You never know who the next Jasper Jones will be."

"That's Jasper Johns, darling," Beatrice Snow corrects her.

"I meant Johns." Candace is not fazed. "Anyway, I love your painting."

"Well, thank you," I say. "You are my first sale."

"That's not quite true," says Beatrice Snow. "She's actually the third. Someone's already purchased the portrait of John Lennon—I knew that one would go—he's always a hot subject and it *is* his birthday—but the George Washington has also been sold."

"*Really?*" It's weird, but my first instinct is to say, no, I'm sorry, but nothing is for sale. I've grown attached to all my paintings and want to keep them forever. Then it sinks in: I am really an artist, and my work is going to be hanging in other people's homes, people I might not ever meet. It is a strange feeling, like they are taking home a piece of me and hanging me on the wall.

"Well, I'd better snatch mine up, then," says Candace, and I think she's made the perfect choice. The painting is of a brunette holding a mirror in the shape of a mask up to her face. Her actual face is pretty, but not beautiful. The face reflected back to her in the mirror is of another woman entirely, bleached blonde, perfect nose, as if she is projecting a completely different image back to herself than who she really is. On the opposite side of the mirror, the mask itself is another face altogether, the face she shows the world. That hair is blond but drab; the features of the mask are exaggerated and false. It's almost as if I painted it for Candace without ever meeting her.

Joe comes back over to us, looking very spiffy in his suit and tie, like he is a foreign dignitary. His eyes are bright. "I want to tell you, Harley, that I am mighty impressed. I felt like the woman with the lion on her shoulder was looking straight into my soul."

"How incredibly poetic." Candace turns to Joe and offers her sparkling hand. "Candace Eastman."

"Joe Walesa." Joe hesitates, then takes Candace's hand.

"Are you a collector?"

"No, ma'am. I drive a cab."

Candace drops Joe's hand as if it were smoldering. She actually wipes her own hand off on her dress. Joe is not daunted; he grins and turns to me. "I should get going, Harley. The missus is probably wondering what happened to me."

I give him a kiss on the cheek. "Thanks, Joe. For everything." Joe starts toward the door. I realize he didn't even charge me for my fare. "Wait," I say. I dig into my purse and take out my sketch pad. I flip to a drawing I sketched a couple of days ago of an older woman, arms outstretched, presenting a huge turkey on a silver platter to an older man sitting at a table with a napkin draped around his neck. Again, I get the feeling that I sketched it for Joe before I even met him. I tear the drawing out of the sketch pad. I take a charcoal out of the box. "What's your wife's name?"

Joe is startled. "Sonja."

I turn the drawing over and write: "For Joe and Sonja. Blessings, Harley Columba." I have already put my signature on the front. I hand the drawing to Joe. "For you. And your wife."

Joe takes the drawing. He holds it in front of himself for a long moment, and then looks back at me, his eyes watery. "I'll get this framed tomorrow. Thank you, honey."

I smile. "You're welcome." As he walks out the door with the drawing under his arm, I think how happy I am to know a piece of me will be hanging on his wall.

I have met so many people that my jaw hurts from smiling. Maybe this is why Beatrice Snow whitens her teeth; they are always exposed. There is a beautiful ballad playing over the loudspeakers about a woman named Mary on Mulberry Avenue, just a simple guitar with the vocal. Everyone really seems to adore my paintings, *dahling*, really, and I am getting all sorts of ideas for new work.

People with sharp angles for bodies, not round and human, but metallic and robotic. Push the button on their back like a talking doll and out come pre-programmed sentences: "Dahling!" "Mahvelous!" "Where do you get your ideas?" Clichés floating in cartoon bubbles. Triangle faces. Rectangle elbows. A connected mass of angles. Interlocking primary colors, only primary colors: bright blue, vivid red, burning yellow. One soft human in the center composed of the colors of nature, listening. Listening. Birds floating in the air dropping number nines from their beaks.

I am chatting with some fellow from the Smithsonian Institution in Washington like I do this every night. I am in the middle of the zillionth telling of where I get my ideas when I feel a hand on my shoulder and hear a voice say, "Excuse me, Harley." I turn, expecting another curator or art critic, but instead look straight into the merry eyes of Sofia from the Eternity shop.

"Sofia!" For a moment, I am confused to see her here, as if she has wandered in from a part of my life that doesn't match this venue. Then the confusion turns to joy and I give her a big hug. "What are you doing here?"

"I thought I'd come surprise you. And I wanted to get out of Lenape." Sofia is dressed in a straight green dress, elegant and sophisticated, heels, and a single ruby around her neck. She introduces a man next to her. "This is my friend Armando."

Armando has black hair and a very dark tan. His green eyes are the color of Sofia's dress, and he looks like the perfect accessory. He is gorgeous in a white suit, and I am surprised that I am not exactly thrilled to see Sofia show up with a man. He lifts my hand and kisses it. "Pleased to meet you, Harley." He has a slight accent; I think he might be from South America.

"Thank you for coming all the way out here," I say.

"Oh, it's not far for me. I live on the Upper West Side." Armando smiles and, I swear, his teeth are as white as Beatrice Snow's. I think everybody in Manhattan is bleaching their teeth.

"Well, then thanks for coming all the way *down* here."

"I enjoy exhibits. I don't know much about art, but I like the chitchat and the wine." Armando looks over at the bar. "Speaking of which, can I get you something to drink? Our scene will not be complete unless we are holding glasses in our hands."

I've already had two flutes of champagne; I think I'd better switch to sparkling water. "Something with bubbles, please, and no alcohol." I'd better watch it; I almost turned into a primary color myself and said "dahling."

Armando does a little bow and makes his way over to the table where the drinks are. "He's gorgeous," I say to Sofia.

"He's just a friend. He's in fashion." Sofia laughs. "Not that I mean South American men are in vogue these days, but that Armando actually works in the fashion business." She glances around the room. "Where's your father?"

"Working. He couldn't get away."

Sofia looks disappointed. "That's too bad. Are you here all alone?"

I indicate the roomful of people. "Except for all of them, yes."

Sofia smiles, but her eyes are concerned. "You know what I mean." She takes my chin in her hand and turns my face toward her. "Are you okay? You look a little sad."

"Do I?" My voice breaks; her words have exposed a crack in my veneer.

"I'm sure I'm the only one who notices. Especially since you're wearing that dress. It's perfect."

I lower my voice. "Oh, Sofia. It's just . . ." I look around the room. "Let's go over in the corner."

We move to an empty corner next to a blank white wall and stand facing each other, our backs to the crowd. Sofia waits, her eyes quizzical. I might as well just come right out and say it: "I think I'm pregnant."

If Sofia is shocked, she doesn't show it. Her voice is calm. "How long?"

"My period is five days late."

"That's not long. It could be stress. Stress has a nasty

habit of scaring periods away." She is pragmatic, and it is like an embrace. "Did you take a pregnancy test?"

"I've been trying all day." I manage a smile. "It's a long story, but during the last attempt the test fell in the toilet and self-destructed."

"Okay, then. Let's not panic. We can stop and buy another test after the exhibit."

I hesitate. "That's not everything. . . . It's . . . well, it's Evan. When I told him, he just flat out refused to have the baby. He refused to even talk about it."

Sofia frowns. "That doesn't sound like Evan."

"We were having a fight about Sean, and I sort of blurted it out in front of our friends. It was probably not the best time to tell him. But I think we were really fighting about something else."

"What?"

"That he is not the most important thing in my life." When the words tumble out of my mouth, I realize I am speaking the truth. "That I don't blindly worship and adore him the way Jessie reveres Oliver. That this . . ." I sweep my arm around my paintings in the room. "That this is just as important. He said I idolized Sean. He sounded jealous."

"Do you love him?" What is nice about Sofia is that she doesn't treat me like I am unqualified to have a valid emotion just because I'm sixteen.

"Yes, I love him; I love him very much. It's just . . ." I hesitate. "My music is changing . . . his is, too. Except it's splitting in different directions. I don't know why, but I keep wanting to listen to Bach and Mozart and opera. He's getting into harsher and more discordant stuff." A group of people burst into laughter on the other side of the room, as if they were eavesdropping and I have said something ridiculous. I lower my voice. "And I'm tired of going to clubs named Hades. I'm tired of the groupies and the phonies and all the posing. It's fun every so often, but not every night." A saxophone starts wailing, and now the song is about how this girl keeps promising to leave but never does. "You know, some girl climbed onstage and tried to wedge her eyes open with toothpicks a couple of months ago? How freaky is that? But Evan is a drummer. That is his *job*. Do you understand? It's who he is. And he's really good; his band is really good. Everyone thinks it's only a matter of time before they hit. And the more successful he becomes, the worse it's going to get."

Sofia nods. "Not the best circumstances to have a baby."

"Yeah. I was thinking the same thing." My eyes get wistful. "I don't even know where he is right now. Oh, it's just so sad."

Sofia puts her arm on my shoulder. "Yeah, it stinks. It's not—" Abruptly, Sofia stops speaking. I watch her eyes focus somewhere over my shoulder. She brightens and says: "Well, hello!" to someone behind me.

"There you are, Harley!" I turn and see my father, Sean Shanahan, standing there, grinning like an errant schoolboy who decided to show up in class. Next to him is Gloria Mason, the understudy, and all her cleavage.

I am so glad to see Sean that I forget that I am furious with him. "Dad! You made it!" I throw my arms around his neck and kiss him.

Sean chuckles, a little awkwardly, but he hugs me back. I realize, then, that it is the first time I have ever called him "Dad." As we embrace, the hug turns from something polite to something intense and the next thing I know we are nearly squeezing the life out of each other. The embrace speaks without words. The embrace says: I'm sorry. I forgive you. I love you. You are my daughter. You are my father.

After a long moment, we finally break apart. Our blue eyes are glistening with tears. I see that Sofia's eyes, too, are moist. Gloria, on the other hand, has her back to us and is checking out the crowd. Sean lightens the moment. "Looks like you got the same bunch that was at the John Lennon show this morning, and then some."

I follow his lead and keep it light. "God, was that only this morning? It seems like a year ago. I was worried that my show would be a disaster. What a waste of energy."

Sean puts his arm around me and gives me another squeeze. "I'm very proud." He turns to Sofia. I watch their eyes connect. "And here's another surprise." He smiles at Sofia as if she were gift wrapped. By the look on her face, the feeling is mutual.

"Aren't you going to introduce me, Sean?" Gloria has turned around and wedges herself between them.

Sean glances at Gloria as if he forgot he had brought her, but he is polite. "Of course. Excuse me. Sofia, this is Gloria. Gloria, Sofia. There's a pair of musical names."

I look at the two women. They couldn't be more different, Gloria with her plunging neckline and short skirt, and Sofia, sophisticated in green. Sofia offers her hand. "Pleased to meet you."

"Likewise," says Gloria. "I'm dying for a drink." She speaks to no one in particular. "As predicted, Josephine was late. And Melanie behaved badly. I beared the brunt of it."

"Gloria's a bit of a drama queen." Sean winks at Sofia.

Gloria takes this as a compliment. "Yeah, well, it comes with the job."

At that moment, Armando arrives with two glasses of red wine balanced in one hand and a glass of Perrier in the other. He looks from Sofia to Sean and then to Gloria. "New arrivals? May I offer you some wine?" He hands me the glass of Perrier. "I have to say, Harley, that even though I'm a total amateur when it comes to art, I'm very impressed."

"Thanks." I take the glass.

"I'll have that glass of red," Gloria says. She turns co-quettish. "As long as you're offering."

"Of course." Armando gives her a glass and hands the other one to Sofia. "Sofia only drinks red. Right?"

Sofia nods. "You know me well."

I step in and make all the introductions. "Armando, this is my father, Sean Shanahan, and Gloria Mason. She's an understudy at my father's show."

"Darling, it's impolite to introduce someone as an understudy." Gloria tosses her head and strikes a pose. "I am an actress!" She uses a theatrical voice and everyone laughs.

Sean and Armando shake hands, and Armando does his kissing number to Gloria's hand. Gloria giggles. She puts on a Southern accent. "A gentleman! It's been a long time since I've met a gentleman!"

I think Gloria has tossed a little dig at Sean, but he is still gazing at Sofia, who is gazing back at him. Neither one of them appears to be listening to Gloria. Armando, in the meantime, has fixated his eyes on Gloria's cleavage. Then they all start talking at the same time, Sean to Sofia and Armando to Gloria. I am barely listening; I am watching the dynamics. There is a subtle shift in position, with Armando moving next to Gloria, bumping Sean over to Sofia.

Beatrice Snow joins our group. "Harley. Sorry to interrupt, but New York Nine has just arrived and they want to interview you." New York Nine is the local television news channel.

I am stunned. "You're kidding."

"No, my dear, I am quite serious. I hope you haven't drunk too much champagne!"

"No, no. I'm fine." I turn to Sean. "This is Beatrice Snow, Sean. She's the owner of the gallery. Beatrice, this is my father, Sean Shanahan."

Beatrice Snow perks up at the mention of Sean's name. "So you managed to make it after all. Good. Good. I'm sure New York Nine would like to interview you, too. Come on. Over here, over by the entry for Life Never Stops."

Sean protests. "No, no. This is Harley's show."

Actually, I would feel a lot better if Sean went on TV with me; I am nervous about doing it alone. "I would love it, Dad," I say. "Please?"

Sean looks at me. I think he can tell I am sincere. "Okay."

Beatrice Snow leads us over to where that really cute newscaster guy on New York Nine is standing with a microphone, eating hors d'oeuvres. I can't believe I am going to be on television. He puts down his plate when Beatrice Snow makes the introduction. "Kirk Daniels, Harley Columba."

"Hey there," says Kirk Daniels, wiping his fingers on a napkin. "Everybody ready? Let's do it. I just got word they need me down by the pier, so, unfortunately, I've got to run." I think it must be a strange life, chasing events as they happen, even stranger than being a drummer in a rock-and-roll band. I wonder if Kirk Daniels is married and how his wife feels about his job.

After that, things move so quickly I don't have time to think. Kirk positions Beatrice Snow and me next to my painting. The cameraman aims his lens at us. The next thing I know, a bright light clicks on and Kirk Daniels starts speaking.

"Good evening. Tonight we are at the opening of the Harley Columba exhibit at Beatrice Snow's gallery in Chelsea. Harley is this month's winner of the Most Promising Young Artist competition."

Then Kirk Daniels sticks the microphone in front of Beatrice Snow's shiny white teeth. She indicates my paintings behind her and starts talking about the competition and the Emily Harvey memorial. "At the end of the year, the winning artist receives a cash prize of five thousand dollars, plus an all-expense-paid trip to Venice, Italy, during its Biennale and a showing at my gallery there." She steps back and points to my entry, the pregnant angel singing down to the pregnant girl inside a tree. "We are standing in front of Harley Columba's submission." She describes what she likes about the painting, using words like "return to timeless classical technique" and "symbolizes" and "harmonious use of color." She sees things that I never knew were there, and it seems like she knows more about my painting than I do.

Kirk Daniels brings the microphone up to his own lips. The next thing I know, he is turning to me and asking me a question. "Harley, how does it feel to be in a celebrated art gallery at such a young age?"

He sticks the microphone in front of my mouth. I have no time to panic; I just start speaking. "It feels good, but surreal, like I'm living someone else's life. It's a real honor and a privilege to be here."

"Your father, the scenic designer Sean Shanahan, is with us tonight." Sean steps up next to me. Kirk Daniels turns to Sean. "You won the Tony last year for *Tall Tales*, and you've got *Answers*, the new Nicholas Raftner play, opening next week. Talent must run in the family."

Sean laughs. He is completely at ease in front of the camera. "I only can say that I am very, very proud of my daughter. To stand here in this room and see all her paintings together in one place, well, it's overwhelming. She's incredibly sophisticated for someone so young. I admire and respect not only her talent but also her vision. She's a very special person, and it is an honor to be her father."

Then, I don't know what comes over me, but I find myself stepping up to the microphone. "The feeling is mutual," I say, and my eyes get teary.

Now Beatrice Snow steps back up to the mike. She talks to Kirk. "In fact, he admires his daughter's work so much, he called ahead and bought a marvelous portrait of George Washington before the show opened tonight."

As my mouth drops open, the cameraman swings the camera over to the portrait of George Washington, mutineers splayed across his forehead. Beatrice Snow starts talking about "originality" and "new perspective to common themes." Sean and I look at each other. I mouth the words "thank you," and he mouths back "no, thank *you*." When we look up, we realize the television camera has focused back on us and caught the moment, and we both smile.

Now Kirk turns and speaks directly to the camera. "A very special father-daughter act, indeed. The Harley Columba exhibit will be running through November 9th. From Chelsea, I'm Kirk Daniels for New York Nine."

The little light on the camera goes out. I feel like I just visited another planet and tumbled back to earth.

The evening is winding to completion, with only a handful of stragglers munching limp hors d'oeuvres and sipping down the wine. Beatrice Snow said I could select what music I wanted to hear, so I picked Glenn Gould playing Bach on the piano. A couple of people from my new school have dropped by, which is really sweet, especially since one of them is this cute boy named Lucien. He is from France and is totally gorgeous, with trendy locks and these kind of golden eyes. His white cotton shirt looks tailor-made; he has a blue polka-dot handkerchief in his pocket for effect. He says "zee" instead of "the"; it's so charming. He is in my creative-writing class, and after this encounter—after this entire *day*—I am definitely rewriting my autobiographical incident paper.

We are having a discussion about Marcel Proust and whether he is better read out loud in front of others or silently alone. Lucien went to the all-day Proust Fest over at the Mercantile Library this past summer on Proust's birthday, and he says it was fantastic. A bunch of writers and celebrities read Proust before an audience with the words projected on a screen. "Eet's like watching a movie, only zee movie is in your head." I have never met anybody else who liked Proust; maybe it's because he's French. I love his nose; it's dignified and elegant, and his face would make an interesting portrait. I think his father is an ambassador.

"Proust says through grief we come alive," Lucien continues. He wants to be a writer; he is obsessed with tumult. "That zee art of living is making good use of zee people who make us suffer. Without grief we have no opportunity to . . . what is zee word . . . alchemize."

"Okay." I nod. I have thought about these things alone in my room. "If you can change grief into ideas, then it loses some of the power to hurt you." I am determined to hold my own in this conversation even though Peppy and Roger have done their best to pound all original thought into a lump of dough. "But so many times we enjoy it too much; we wallow in it and don't use it for anything productive."

We are in the middle of wondering whether Proust was a genius or insane when I look up and see Evan, Jessie, and Oliver walk through the door. "Harley! We saw you on TV!" Jessie dashes into the gallery and throws her arms around me. I am surprised to realize that with all the excitement I had forgotten about them, but now that they are here, I am happy to see them.

"We were over at this bar and New York Nine was on the tube and all of a sudden, there you were. It was pretty cool." Oliver seems impressed. "It was kind of like a reality show, only it was really real."

I watch Evan examine Lucien, the two of them standing next to each other, the rocker and the sophisticate, black and white. I try to imagine having a conversation about Proust with Evan. I think it would not be possible, although I am certain he knows all about changing grief into ideas. "Hey, Harley," Evan says. He doesn't meet my eyes.

"Hello, Evan. This is Lucien. He goes to school with me." Evan offers Lucien his hand and they shake.

"We were just speaking about Proust," Lucien says, as casually as if we had been discussing the weather. "What do you think? Is eet better to suffer zee pains of love than never to have loved at all? Does jealousy cause you to search more deeply into the character of another, ask questions that you would not normally ask?"

Evan might be a drummer, but he is no dummy, and I am curious how he will answer. "I guess it depends on how much money you've got," he says.

Lucien is a little thrown. "What do you mean?"

"Most people are too busy working their asses off. They don't have time to think those thoughts. But, yeah, if you can afford it, it's better to take a trip into the darkness so that you can appreciate the light. There is nothing worse than being on automatic pilot." Evan pauses. "But, honestly, I don't know who the hell Proust is."

Lucien bursts out laughing. "Good answer. Very Proustian. Only a Proustian would admit they didn't know who Proust was." Evan grins, and I think they could be comrades, despite the difference in their clothes.

Sean wanders over. "Well, today has been some kind of day, October 9th, Harley's ninth." He chuckles. "Harley's Ninth. That sounds like a symphony. How about we all head down to the Village and get a pizza to celebrate?"

"Well . . ." Evan hesitates. "We should get back to New Jersey." He looks at me, as if the decision rests on my shoulders.

I don't know what is going to happen between Evan and me, but there is no reason we can't start from here. I nod. "Come on. It'll be fun."

"You can always crash at my apartment," Sean says. "The sofa pulls out into a bed. Jessie and Oliver could sleep there." He doesn't say where Evan sleeps, but there is only one place for him, and that is my bed.

Evan considers this proposition. "Yes, to the pizza," he says. "But then we have to head back into the Tunnel." He looks right at me. "I've got a lot of stuff I need to do tomorrow."

It is a simple sentence, but it hits me like a dart. There was a time when Evan would have leaped at the opportunity to spend the night in bed with me. I force myself to sound cheery. "Okay, then. Let me just run to the ladies' room." I feel an approaching storm brewing in my eyes, and I don't want to cry in front of everybody. I grab my purse and rush to the back of the gallery.

I push down the brass handle of the bathroom door and enter. The light flickers on automatically. *Blink. Blink. Blink.* It is not one of those fluorescent lights that every bathroom has but the color of a soft rose.

Beatrice Snow's bathroom is stamped with femininity, and I am surprised. There is a pedestal sink on one wall with a curvy mirror above it. In the corner, the toilet is pink; a vase of fresh flowers is centered on the tank. The floor is white tile decorated with hand-painted roses. A white wicker trash basket is next to the sink. On a marble ledge below the mirror are lacy cloth towels for drying your hands.

There are small black-and-white etchings all over the walls of half-naked women in erotic poses. The one next to the mirror is of an elegant woman lolling on a chaise lounge wearing a corset and long gloves past her elbows. The bottom half of her body is nude. The curve of the chaise lounge curls her back into a sitting recline. Her knees are bent up in the air; she wears spiky heels on her feet. Suspended between her ankles is a goose with a little ribbon around its neck, webbed feet dangling. The woman's eyes are closed; her face is serene and confident. There is a black mask toward the bottom of the chaise lounge.

I am riveted by the etching. Then I realize the goose is not a goose at all, but a swan. It is an etching of the Greek myth, Leda and the Swan, when Zeus turned himself into a swan to seduce Leda because she was so beautiful. As I move in for a closer look, I catch my reflection in the mirror. I shift my eyes to my face. My expression is mysterious, even to myself. My eyes are sad, but there are two pinpoints of light emanating from the pupils, as if I have grown wiser. There is a tiny smile on my lips. The expression looks familiar; it nags at me. I feel I've seen it somewhere before, someplace recently. I realize it is the same look that the Madonna of Victory wore inside the church.

I feel weary, suddenly. The events of the day have stacked themselves into a tower ready to collapse. I walk to the toilet and lift my dress. I tug down my black lacy thong. I sit on the toilet and start to pee. When I am finished, I wipe myself. It feels slick. I look down at the toilet paper in my hand. It is streaked with blood.

I have gotten my period.

Creative writing
Mr. Alberti
Room 225
Autobiographical incident

UP ON THE ROOF
by Harley Columba

Again, I go up to the roof. I do this for a reason. I do this
to drive Brad Festerly mad.

You're not supposed to come up here because the
co-op association says so. I go anyway. This is the notice
on the door at the top of the stairs:

YOU ARE TRESPASSING.
VIOLATORS WILL BE PROSECUTED
TO THE FULL EXTENT OF THE LAW.
THIS IS AN EMERGENCY EXIT ONLY.
WHEN ALARM SOUNDS,
POLICE WILL BE CALLED.

I have already trespassed, but I have not forgiven
those who trespassed against me. I want victory. I push
down hard on the red alarm bar on the door. I know no
alarm will sound; I know nothing will happen; it is a
threat that is only real for those who believe in the words.

I have been spying, and I happen to know that the
president of the co-op association, Brad Festerly, is up
here all the time, smoking and watching the Hudson
River. He has the top apartment, and uses the staircase as
his personal storage area for garden supplies and boots,
yet he fined old Bob for putting up Halloween decorations

in the hall. He locked little Nellie's and Jimmy's bicycles down in the basement and put his daughter's stroller under the stairwell instead. He runs around with a portable easel and watercolors and sits in front of Brew Bar on a collapsible stool, copying street scenes, crudely, like a child. He thinks he is an artist, but he is a fraud.

I have my sketch pad with me; I want to work under the spell of the river in the distance, visible through a gap between the buildings. I also carry a mirror. I want to sketch my own face. I have an idea for an oil painting, a goddess of my own creation—a sexy Madonna, a modern Isis, a new Amaterasu, the Japanese sun goddess—and I want to capture the image before it disappears into the vapors of my mind.

I know, also, that my footsteps will alert Brad Festerly, and I want to do my part to enlarge his artistic perspective.

I flip open my sketch pad and take a piece of charcoal out of its case. I prop my sketch pad on the ledge of the building. I sketch a woman reclining in the hollow of a mountaintop. Her hair is long, and shaped as if it is the veil of the Virgin Mary. She has wings, Indian-feather wings. The bottom half of her body is nude. Her knees are bent up in the air. Her feet are bare—with spindly, elegant toes like fingers and semi-circular arches. Suspended between her thighs is a glowing sun; yellow beams shoot out between her legs and into the atmosphere. Inside her womb is a golden egg. The woman's eyes look sideways, right at the viewer. Her eyes are mysterious and wise. There is a tiny smile on her lips, serene and confident. I will call my painting *The Madonna of the Sun.* I am shading her ankles when I hear the fire door slam.

"You again."

I turn to find the voice and look into the sun. I see the silhouette of Brad Festerly, wearing his usual baseball cap.

"Sorry, but I'm trying to concentrate." I turn my gaze again to my charcoal.

"*What* did you say?" He comes close to my shoulder. He is breathing coercion all over me, the color of my charcoal.

My voice is quiet and direct. "I said I'm trying to concentrate. I'm trying to sketch an idea. Did you ever make an oil painting?"

Brad Festerly hesitates, as if this were a trick question. "No . . ."

"Come back and talk to me after you have." I am as surprised as he is to hear these words come out of my mouth.

It is as if I had hit Brad Festerly's self-destruct button; he starts to short-circuit. He opens his mouth to respond. "Why you—" He stops. "That's—" He tries again. "I could—" He sputters and stops, sputters and stops. He makes a fist and releases it. We both know he will never be able to make an oil painting; he can barely make a watercolor. He can only bully, not create. Finally, he spits out: "Go to hell."

I resist the impulse to respond. Instead, I remain silent and continue my charcoal strokes. Stroke. Here is the sun. Stroke. Here is the moon. Stroke. Here is gold. Stroke. Here is silver. Stroke. There is the river. Stroke. Here is the tree. Stroke. There is the sky. Stroke. Stroke. Stroke.

Brad Festerly watches me for a long moment. I can feel him try to burn me with his eyes. "You no good . . ."

He starts hollering and yelling, but I turn down the volume until I can no longer hear his words. I can only hear the prehistoric birds flying through the sky, singing and chortling and whistling. I am sure that one day I will be able to break the code of the birds if only I listen long enough.

Finally, Brad Festerly surrenders and walks back to the fire door. He pushes it open. He exits, stage left.

The door closes softly, silently behind him.

Questions Answered

By FRANK POVERO

When a playwright entitles his latest work *Answers,* unless he is prepared to respond with profundity, he sets himself up for assault. Luckily for us, Nicholas Raftner meets this challenge with wisdom and aplomb. Questions are answered, but more importantly, they lead to new questions more interesting than the original queries—questions concerning the dance between the male and female, questions regarding life itself.

He is fortunate enough to work again with Garth Gallo, a director who succeeds in alchemizing his almost mythic language into action and story. When Dagmar, the long-suffering wife of philandering Louis, asks "Why?" Louis is prepared with the answers. Characters which could have appeared stereotypical—certainly the situation they are thrust into is more common than not—have such depth and eccentricity that nearly every ordinary question provides an answer that stuns, and, more importantly, demands that we ponder the reply.

Gloria Mason, in a theatrical coincidence that rivals *All About Eve,* replaced Melanie Sumner as Dagmar on opening night due to a broken leg that Ms. Sumner suffered during a tech rehearsal. Ms. Mason steps into the role of Dagmar as if dragging her own shadow self into the light. Sometimes a child, sometimes a nag, sometimes a harlot—but rarely a wife—Ms. Mason's performance makes it easy to see why Louis seeks solace outside his marriage. Dagmar stabs her hook with different bait—sex, guilt, revenge, jealousy—and Louis, almost resignedly, swallows the lure every time. He yearns to break away, but the pointed arrow seems to have caught him right in the throat.

Louis, played by veteran Chad Lombardy, is equal parts rogue, weakling and weasel, yet so charming and ultimately noble that we understand the reasons why he roams. Still, the answers lead to more questions. Why did he marry Dagmar in the first place? Is she only a trophy, equipped with the required bosom? Or was it an attempt to dominate and fustigate a female after spending his childhood as a replacement husband for his own mother?

If all this sounds tragic, it's not. *Answers* is actually a comedy, albeit along the lines of Dante's *Divina Commedia*. On opening night, after one brilliant gem of a reply, the audience laughed themselves to tears.

Sean Shanahan, who won the Tony last year for set design for *Tall Tales*, provides a haunting backdrop that adds dramatic layers to this poignant story, as does Hank Zippel's lighting design. In one breathtaking scene, the cavernous living room magically transforms into the hull of a boat, achieved miraculously only by the use of light and sound. Anna Poppaea's richly textured costumes add to the effect, and Martyn Ware's otherworldly compositions transport the audience from heaven to hell and then back again.

The rest of the cast, Josephine Warren as Louis' dictatorial mother, Donna; Herb Cox as her muddled husband, wryly named King; and Peggy Wells and Scott Watson as their gossipy neighbors, Ethel and Fred (in an homage to *I Love Lucy*) couldn't be better.

However, it is Ms. Mason and Mr. Lombardy who cement the production in emotional reality, and it is mesmeric to watch their never-ending dance. Rarely have two characters seemed so wrong for each other, yet so unable to break apart. As we watch them tumble deeper into despondency, which can lead to only one place— the grave—we resist the urge to jump onstage and wrench them from each other's arms. *Answers* is a tribute to those among us with enough courage to face the world alone, and a reminder how fortunate we are to be living at a time when a playwright such as Nicholas Raftner exists.

CURRENT PRODUCTION NOTES:
ANSWERS
Playwright: Nicholas Raftner
Director: Garth Gallo
Cast: Gloria Mason (Dagmar), Chad Lombardy (Louis), Josephine Warren (Donna), Herb Cox (King), Peggy Wells (Ethel), Scott Watson (Fred)
Set Design: Sean Shanahan
Lighting Design: Hank Zippel
Costume Design: Anna Poppaea
Sound Design: Alain Arias-Misson
Music Composed and Arranged by Martyn Ware
Running Time: 2 1/2 hours, with intermission
Walter Kerr Theatre
219 West 48th Street
New York
Reviewed by Frank Povero based on October 13 performance

TRADITION IN FLUX
by Malcolm Bryce Emerson
International Tribune
January 22nd

....

At the nucleus of New York's busy art scene in Chelsea, the Beatrice Snow Gallery continued its 7th annual Most Promising Young Artist competition with more talent and artistic diversity than ever, culminating with the current show, which combines the work of the twelve monthly winners from last year in one grand exhibition.

Beatrice Snow's juried show presented works by young talent—under the age of twenty-one—from all over the United States. The work by this year's participating artists was reviewed and selected by Ira Schwartz, executive director of the Apprentice's Art League in New York City, based on the theme Life Never Stops, a phrase originally coined by Fluxus artist Ben Vautier. The topic pays homage to Emily Harvey, a longtime gallery owner and supporter of the arts who died on November 8 and was a good friend of Beatrice Snow.

From the 12 competing artists, Mr. Schwartz selected Harley Columba of New York as exceptional, winning the Most Promising Young Artist award. The 16-year-old artist has the distinction of being the youngest participant to win the prestigious award since the competition started seven years ago. In addition to a cash prize of $5,000, Ms. Columba will receive an all-expense-paid trip to Venice, Italy, for its Biennale in June, and a showing at Beatrice Snow's Venetian gallery.

Harley Columba's magnificent oil painting captured the essence of the theme with startling vision. The piece centers on a young nude woman encased by the Tree of Life, arms overhead, as if she slid into the trunk from the heavens. The young woman is serenely pregnant; the features of the female child inside her womb are visibly similar to the young woman's. Overhead flies the young woman in the form of an angel, also pregnant with the same child. The angel, who has the wings of an eagle, and the young woman sing to each other, embracing each other with a symphony of gently cascading musical notes, one octave ascending, the other descending.

Instead of tongues, the images have licks of flames.

The combination of the Tree of Life with Eros is almost Jungian in its expression and perfectly reflects the Life Never Stops theme. It is a noble memorial for the much-beloved Emily Harvey and a refreshing return to tradition with so many young artists seemingly floundering for a voice.

Ms. Columba said, "The first question I asked is, 'Can this be true?' I feel honored and privileged to win such a prestigious award." When asked how the Fluxus movement had inspired her to create a classic oil painting, Ms. Columba replied, "To be perfectly honest, I am not sure I understand what Fluxus is, though I would like to know more about it. My inspiration was the theme Life Never Stops." Ms. Columba thanked her father, Broadway set designer Sean Shanahan, for "his encouragement and his belief in me," and also her high school art teacher, Emma Posey, and her grandmother, Eliza Tuttle, for their support.

The Beatrice Snow Most Promising Young Artist Competition is an effort to recognize and nurture young artists. The 12 prizewinning entries will be on display at the Beatrice Snow Gallery daily from 11 a.m. to 6 p.m. through the end of January.

Beatrice Snow Gallery
529 West 24th Street
New York
212-555-8080

ACKNOWLEDGMENTS

A heartfelt thank-you to my editor, Joan Slattery, who added joy to my craft, and to the twins, who graciously shared nine months *in utero* with *Harley's Ninth*. Thanks to assistant editor extraordinaire Allison Wortche, and to my agent, William Clark, for his faith and belief. Thank you to Nancy Hinkel, Bill Adams, and everyone at Random House who helped bring my book to life, and to all the agents at Andrew Nurnberg Associates. I am indebted to the Broadway scenic designer David Gallo, who was generous with his time and energy, and, in Italy, to the director Elena Barbalich and to the staff at the Teatro Carlo Goldoni for their help. Thank you to Erin Black, Samara Powell, and Deby Veneziale for their thoughts and feedback, and to Glenn Kitchart for the inspiration. In Venice, special thanks to Nicoletta Vettore, Sergio Boldrin, Andrea and Margherita Castione, Nicolò Cristante, and Emanuela Brusegan, and to Geoff and Liz Leckie for giving me a new appreciation for oil and canvas. Thanks also to Roberto Silva for his fantastic photos, and to the cover artist, Philippe Lardy, who transformed the power of the words into images and symbols. Much appreciation goes to Jenny de Jonge at Gottmer for her insight, and to Bob and Karen Bauer, Michael Goldfarb, Christin Cockerton, and Romola Vivien for their hospitality and smiles. Also, I am grateful to my sisters, Linda, Sharon, and Kim, for the supplies, the support, and all the roses.

HARLEY's NINTH

Cat Bauer's first novel, *Harley, Like a Person*, was named an American Library Association Best Book for Young Adults, an ALA Quick Pick for Reluctant Readers, and an ALA Popular Paperback. It was also selected as a *Booklist* Top 10 First Novel for Youth and a Book Sense 76 Pick, and won the Society of Children's Book Writers and Illustrators Sue Alexander Most Promising New Work Award. The author continues Harley's story in this companion novel, *Harley's Ninth*.

Cat Bauer grew up in New Jersey, and has also lived in New York City and Los Angeles. She now lives in Venice, Italy, where she has been a regular contributor to such publications as the *International Herald Tribune*'s Italian supplement. To learn more about the author and her work, please visit her Web site at www.catbauer.com.